The Solomon Scroll

by

Alex Lukeman

CHAPTER 1

The train was almost ready to leave.

Professor Angelo Caprini settled down on the seat of his first-class compartment and wrinkled his nose at a faint hint of perfume left behind by the previous occupant. He glanced at the bag resting next to him. The contents were going to make him famous.

Caprini was a short man, squat. He had a prosperous gut that spilled out over his belt. His eyes bulged behind thick glasses, an effect made worse by a receding chin. Behind his back his colleagues called him The Frog. It was an apt description, right down to the hint of webbing between his toes, although no one but Caprini knew about that.

He'd spent the last three days at the European Synchrotron Radiation Facility in Grenoble, the holy grail for researchers seeking the most advanced x-ray technology in the world. The bag contained an ancient scroll from the Roman town of Herculaneum, destroyed along with Pompeii by the eruption of Mount Vesuvius in 79 CE. The scroll was unreadable, encased in a hardened shell of black volcanic ash. Caprini had made the pilgrimage to Grenoble hoping that advances in crystal x-ray phase tomography could reveal the charcoal-based ink on the burned papyrus concealed beneath the crust of lava. His faith had been rewarded.

The scroll came from the library of the Villa Literati in Herculaneum, the only collection of written works surviving from the ancient world.

There were hundreds of scrolls but no one knew what secrets they concealed. A lost work by Plato, perhaps. A firsthand account of the Punic wars. A play by Aristotle. A contemporary account of the crucifixion of Christ. Anything was possible.

Caprini could barely contain his excitement when the x-rays revealed the first page, white lines of Aramaic lettering against a black background. Parts of the second page could be seen under the first, faint ghosts written down two thousand years before. While the technician operated the equipment, Caprini couldn't keep himself from talking about what he was seeing.

The tech had a profitable agreement to pass on information when something of unusual interest turned up at the research facility. Listening to Caprini babble on, the technician knew the scroll was something that qualified. A few days after leaving a message money would appear in his Swiss bank account. The more important the message, the more money appeared. It was a very satisfactory arrangement. The technician had made the call after he got off work.

Impatient, Caprini tapped his foot on the floor of the train compartment. He was looking forward to getting back to Naples and his wife's cooking, proper food, not like here in France. The food in France was too rich, it always gave him indigestion. He'd be in Rome tomorrow morning and by afternoon, back in Naples at his office at the National Museum where he could organize his notes and plan his announcement.

If I wasn't afraid of flying I'd be there by now, he thought. He glanced again at the overnight bag. The scroll was inside, safely tucked away in a hard case with a bed of foam.

A man in a conductor's uniform knocked on the compartment door. He held a brown, paper wrapped package in his hand.

"Yes?"

"*Professore* Caprini?"

"Yes, what is it?"

"There is a package for you, sir."

That's odd, Caprini thought. He opened the door, reaching for the package. The conductor took a silenced pistol from under his uniform coat and fired twice. Caprini looked down at his chest in shock. The assassin caught him before he fell, then propped the body up in the corner of the seat. Small spots of blood showed on the front of the professor's blue Armani suit.

The assassin pulled the curtains of the private compartment closed. He placed the package on an overhead shelf, picked up Caprini's overnight bag and looked inside. He opened the case containing the scroll. Satisfied, he closed the bag, backed out of the compartment and shut the door behind him. If anyone looked in, they'd think the professor was asleep.

The train was about to leave. Caprini's killer stepped back onto the platform and walked away into the milling crowd.

Some time later the train was crossing a deep gorge in the Italian Alps when the package detonated and ripped apart Professor Caprini's coach. The blast sent the speeding train off the rails, to its doom.

The screams of the passengers echoed from the indifferent walls of the gorge.

The train fell for a long time until it smashed onto the rocks far below.

CHAPTER 2

It was another scorching summer on the East Coast. Waves of heat shimmered off the surface of the highway. Nick Carter thought about the cabin he'd once had in California. It had been cool there in the Sierra foothills, dry, a far cry from the steaming humidity of Virginia.

The cabin was gone, burned to the ground. Nick hadn't decided if he wanted to rebuild it but if he did, it wouldn't be any time soon. There were other things on his mind. Like the wedding to Selena Connor they never seemed to schedule. Like the loft they'd just bought overlooking the Potomac. Like whatever the reason was that Director Harker had called him in. There'd been a time when he'd looked forward to a new assignment. Now he was beginning to dread what another mission might bring.

Maybe it's time to get out, he thought. Then, *Who are you kidding? What else are you going to do?*

He pulled into the parking lot in front of the Project Headquarters building, shut down the engine, got out and walked across the hot pavement to the entrance. Nick entered his personal code and placed his right eye in front of the scanner. He waited for the electronic gods that controlled the steel door to recognize him and grant entrance. The door clicked open. Cool air greeted him inside. He breathed a sigh of relief.

The Project was the brainchild of President Rice, small, independent of the rest of America's intelligence network. It was funded by a black budget and controlled by the White House. An angry senator had once described it as the president's personal hit team. Sometimes Nick thought that wasn't far from the truth.

The headquarters building was located in Virginia, within commuting distance of the Capitol. It had the look of an upscale country ranch home surrounded by lawns, trees and flowerbeds.

Looks were deceiving.

The house was built over a Cold War missile site. The missiles with their promise of the end of the world were long gone. The old magazines below the green lawns now housed an armory and shooting range, an operations center, comfortable emergency quarters and a room filled with Cray computers and advanced communications equipment. There was even a swimming pool, courtesy of the previous owners, millionaire survivalists who'd feared a coming apocalypse. The lawns triggered alarms if anything threatening walked over them. Cameras watched everything.

There was a wide, paved parking lot in front of the house. A low building that looked like a warehouse squatted across the way. A hardened concrete helicopter pad anchored the end of the parking lot. From the lot, the drive disappeared over a rise until it reached a chain-link fence surrounding the property and a manned guardhouse at the entrance.

Nick made his way to Harker's office. The rest of the team was already there.

Elizabeth Harker tapped her fingers on the hard surface of her desk as he came in. She gave him one of her warning looks.

Harker was a small woman but she gave off enough energy for someone a lot bigger. Her hair was jet black, streaked with white. She had startling green eyes that stood out against milk white skin. One of her looks of displeasure felt like it could cut to the bone. She wore a tailored black pants suit with a white blouse. A diamond pin in the shape of a swan graced her jacket.

"We're not interrupting your day, are we? Because if we are we could just do this tomorrow."

"Sorry, Director. Traffic."

Selena sat on a couch in front of Harker's desk, next to Ronnie Peete. She'd left the loft before him. Nick sat down next to her.

"Hey," she said.

"Hey."

"Yah t'a hey, Nick," Ronnie said.

Ronnie was Navajo, raised on the big reservation. He looked as though he could have stepped out of a Frederick Remington painting, although Remington probably wouldn't have painted his subject in a bright Hawaiian shirt. He and Nick went back a long way, to Iraq and Afghanistan and the jungles of Colombia. Both had been Marine Recon before they'd come to the Project.

Selena had never been in the military. She'd found herself recruited into the Project almost by accident. What she lacked in military experience she made up for with plenty of skills that filled out the team. An expert in ancient languages, she was athletic, smart and independent. She was also rich, a legacy from her uncle. His death had brought her to Nick, Elizabeth and the others.

She was two inches shorter than Nick's muscular six feet and sixty pounds shy of his two hundred. Her eyes were an unusual color, mostly violet, sometimes blue. There was a dark mole above her lip. Her hair was feathered back on the sides, longer in back, a natural reddish blonde. One of her cheekbones was a little higher than the other, giving her face an attractive, asymmetric appeal. Selena moved with unconscious ease that hinted at her athletic ability. Like Nick, there was a hint of something feral about her, something held in check. She looked as if she could explode into motion in an instant.

Elizabeth said, "I have a candidate to replace Lamont."

"Big shoes," Ronnie said. "Feels weird not to have him sitting here."

"No one fills Lamont's shoes. If this man works out he'll bring his own."

Lamont Cameron had been badly wounded on the last mission, enough to convince him it was time to quit. It was the first time a core member of the team had decided to hang it up, a reminder that they were all getting older. It was becoming harder to stay in shape for what they had to do. Harder to survive people trying to kill them, which happened with unpleasant frequency.

"What's his name, this candidate?" Nick asked.

"Diego Ramirez." Elizabeth pushed a folder across her desk. "Here's his jacket."

"What's the short version?"

"Rangers, Special Ops. Two tours in Afghanistan, one in Iraq. Purple Heart, Bronze Star with V."

"What outfit?"

"75th Ranger Regiment."

"Those guys are good," Ronnie said.

"When does he get here?" Nick asked.

"This afternoon at 1300. I want you to begin with him right away. Get him oriented. Test him out. I want a full evaluation in three days. If you want him, we'll make it official. He's not happy about coming here. I know he has the skills but I don't know if he's got the attitude we need to be a good fit."

"Sounds like a challenge," Ronnie said. "How old is this guy?"

"Twenty-seven."

"A kid," Ronnie said.

"Rank?"

"Staff Sergeant."

"That says a lot at his age," Nick said. "Is there anything else, Director? If not, we'll go get things ready for him."

"No, that's it for now."

Outside the house, the three of them looked at each other.

"A new guy," Selena said.

"Army," Ronnie said.

"This is going to be interesting," Nick said.

CHAPTER 3

"Here he comes," Ronnie said.

Ronnie, Selena and Nick stood outside Project Headquarters waiting for their new recruit. A shiny red Dodge Challenger R/T came toward them down the drive. Dust rose behind it.

"Moving right along. You can tell something about people from the kind of car they drive," Nick said.

"What does his car tell you?" Selena asked.

"He thinks he's a hotshot. That car has almost 500 horses."

"My old Mercedes had more than that," Selena said, "before the Chinese trashed it. Does that make me a hotshot?"

"No, just hot."

Selena punched him in the arm.

"Smartass."

"Hey, that was a compliment."

The car parked facing the house. The man who got out was about the same height as Ronnie, with the kind of wide shoulders and muscled arms that showed he spent a lot of time working out. He had black hair cropped short to his skull. A few acne scars marked his face. His ears were small and close to his head. His nose looked like it might have been broken sometime in the past. Ramirez wore aviator style sunglasses that concealed his eyes.

His walk was confident as he came toward them but Nick could see wariness in the way he moved. It was a familiar look in Special Forces. Ramirez wasn't going to give anything away.

"Diego Ramirez," he said. "Am I in the right place? I expected something a little more impressive, like CIA or something."

He held out his hand. Nick took it. Ramirez exerted a little too much pressure.

Let the games begin, Nick thought.

"Nick Carter. You're in the right place, Sergeant. What you see isn't necessarily what you get. This is Ronnie Peete and Selena Connor."

"Where's the rest of your team?"

"You're looking at it."

Ramirez started to say something, thought better of it.

"You look familiar. Aren't you the guy that was in Jerusalem with the president a few years back?"

"That's me. Let's go inside."

The events in Jerusalem had brought Nick his fifteen minutes of fame. Saving the president's ass on world TV would do that for you, but he could have done without it.

Elizabeth was waiting for them with Stephanie Willits. Steph was Elizabeth's deputy, in charge of keeping the big Crays on the lower level happy. She had broken into the Pentagon servers at the ripe age of eighteen. When the FBI showed up at the door of her parents' suburban home she'd chosen to work for the NSA rather than go to prison. Elizabeth had lured her away a few years later.

Steph was in her late twenties. A casual glance saw an average looking woman with a pleasant face. A more careful look told a deeper story. Her brown eyes were alive and vibrant, her hair a lustrous dark brown color that reached to her shoulders. She wore large gold earrings. A half dozen gold bracelets circled her left wrist. Stephanie wasn't slim but she wasn't a large woman either.

Today she wore a loosely belted blue dress that fell easily to her knees.

Nick liked Stephanie. They all did. Lately she'd seemed happier than usual. She was engaged to Lucas Monroe, a rising star at Langley. Nick had a high regard for Lucas, something he reserved for few people.

"Sergeant Ramirez, welcome to the Project," Elizabeth said. "I'm Director Harker. You've met Nick, Ronnie and Selena. This is my deputy, Stephanie Willits."

"Hello, Sergeant," Steph said.

"Ma'am."

"Take a seat." Elizabeth gestured at the couch and chairs in front of her desk. Ramirez sat down.

Elizabeth looked at her new potential team member. Ramirez was sitting uncomfortably on one end of the couch, his back straight.

"You can relax, Sergeant. I'm not going to bite."

"No, ma'am."

His shoulders loosened, just a little.

"Don't call me ma'am, Sergeant. I'm not a schoolteacher. Call me Director." She paused. "I understand that you did not want this assignment. Is that correct?"

"With all due respect, Director, no I didn't. I'm not a spook."

"We're not spooks, as you put it," Harker said. "I prefer to think of us as problem solvers. Our unit serves at the pleasure of the president. We can do things that others can't. Tell me, why did you volunteer for the Rangers?"

Nick watched Ramirez. Harker's question caught him by surprise but his answer was immediate.

"Because it's a damn good outfit, the best."

"That's the only reason?"

"It was the main reason. I wanted to serve my country."

"You have combat experience," Elizabeth said. "What we do isn't like what you're used to but there are times when that experience is going to come in handy. If you make the team, you'll find that out."

"If?" Ramirez said.

"Oh, I'm sorry, did you think your assignment here was permanent? That's only if you get through our evaluation. You're on temporary duty until further notice. Stephanie will get you set up in quarters downstairs so you don't have to leave the area. She'll take retinal scans and prints and enter you into the security system. Nick is team leader and your commander in the field. He's in charge of your training."

Nick said, "After you get settled in, we'll begin with a full workout this afternoon. Tomorrow we'll see how you do in hand-to-hand combat. Selena will be in charge of that."

Ramirez looked at Selena. She gave him a sweet expression.

"Are you serious? That's not exactly fair. I was battalion champion in hand-to-hand."

"Then maybe you can show me some moves," Selena said.

"Sure. I'll go easy on you."

Ronnie looked down at his feet and tried not to laugh.

CHAPTER 4

Early the next morning Nick took the team and Ramirez for a run around the property. If Ramirez was surprised by the pace Nick set or by Selena's easy ability to keep it up, he didn't show it. Nick put on a sudden spurt at the end. Selena sprinted past Ramirez until she came even with Nick. They reached the house together, Ronnie and Ramirez close behind.

They went down to the lower level under the house and into the workout room.

"Five minutes," Nick said. "There's water in that refrigerator, Sergeant."

He walked over to Selena. "Give him the works," he said. "Don't hurt him."

"I'll try not to but sometimes people get overenthusiastic."

"Just don't do any permanent damage."

A few minutes later Selena and Ramirez stood on opposite sides of a large mat. Elizabeth and Stephanie had come into the room to watch. They took seats by the wall.

"Okay," Nick said. "Sergeant, I want you to try and take Selena down. Selena, don't let him. No lethal blows. Aside from that, no rules."

Ramirez looked at him. "She could get hurt," he said.

"That's her problem. Don't hold back. Ready?"

They both nodded.

"Begin."

Selena waited to see if Ramirez would bow. He nodded but he didn't bow. They both advanced to the middle of the mat. Ramirez attacked with a combination kick and elbow strike. He was fast, but Selena wasn't where the blows were supposed to land. She swept his leg aside, blocked his strike and landed a kick to his hip that staggered him to the edge of the mat.

He came back and tried a high kick to her head. She moved. His foot swept harmlessly past her face. She grabbed his leg as it went by, stepped to the side and used his momentum to flip him onto his back. Ramirez landed hard and grunted. He bounced up and began circling. There was a new awareness in his eyes as he watched her. His face was getting red.

The next minutes repeated what had gone before. Each time Ramirez attacked, Selena blocked or avoided his strikes and threw him to the mat. He barely touched her with all his attempts. After the last fall, Ramirez got up and looked at her with something different in his expression.

Selena saw that he was losing discipline and meant to teach her a lesson. She decided to end it. He came in and faked a kick, followed by a strike to a nerve center under the collar bone. If it had landed, the fight would have been over and Selena would have been hurt. She leaned back with smooth motion born of more than twenty years of practice. As the strike went by she pivoted and grabbed his right arm. She pulled it down and behind and up at the same time, turning the arm at an odd angle.

Ramirez yelled out in pain. He went to his knees.

"Don't move," Selena said. "If you move, your shoulder will dislocate. The tendons will tear. You don't want that. Have you had enough?"

Ramirez gritted his teeth and tensed.

"I mean it. Don't move."

"Enough," he said.

Selena released the lock, stepped away and bowed.

"Damn it," Ramirez said. He gripped his shoulder.

"Hurts, doesn't it?" Selena said.

Ramirez stood up, rubbing his shoulder. He looked at Selena. Then he bowed. She inclined her head.

"Good," Nick said. "What did you do wrong, Sergeant?"

Ramirez thought. He looked down at his feet, then looked up again.

"I got angry. I wanted to teach her a lesson."

"That's the first thing. Anger clouds your judgement. You can't let it take over. What else?"

"I underestimated her."

"That's right. Why did you do that?"

"I never thought any woman could beat me."

"Now you know they can. It's not just weapons that make women dangerous. Sometimes we go places where the women are worse than the men. You'd better remember it. You should know that, you were in Afghanistan."

Ramirez had the grace to look embarrassed. "I won't forget."

"For what it's worth, you never had a chance," Nick said. "Selena can beat any one of us. Probably anyone you've ever met, including your instructors. She's thrown me down on that mat so many times I can't even remember. But you can learn from her, if you're willing to."

"Copy that," Ramirez said. "What's next?"

"I'll give you an hour to ice that shoulder and let it calm down. There's some aspirin in the bathroom cabinet if you want it. Then we hit the range," Nick said. "Then the urban combat course in the building across the lot."

At the end of the day, Nick stopped by Elizabeth's office on the way out.

"How's the new guy doing?" she asked.

"Not bad. He can shoot, no doubt about that. He was kind of embarrassed about what happened with Selena."

Elizabeth smiled. "See you at the briefing tomorrow morning."

After Nick left the room she leaned back in her chair, thinking about Ramirez. She hoped he would work out. She was fortunate she hadn't needed to break in someone new before now. Over the years there had been plenty of injuries, plenty of close calls for everyone, herself included.

For Elizabeth, the Project team was her family. She'd been married, once. Before the president tapped her to head up the Project she'd worked in the Justice Department. She'd thought she'd found the perfect partner in a coworker who became her husband. That ended when he chose political advancement and a wealthy socialite lover over her.

Elizabeth had given up on the idea that she'd find someone to share her life with. There would be no family in the traditional sense of the word. Nick, Selena, Stephanie and the others had become her family. Now there was a new addition with Ramirez.

I could do worse, she thought.

CHAPTER 5

Nick lifted the lid from a pan simmering on the stove. He stirred, inhaling the spicy odor of the food. He looked out the kitchen window at the setting sun, dark red in the humid, smog filled air over the Potomac. Inside the loft it was cool, pleasant. Miles Davis played in the background.

"A few more minutes," he said.

Selena stood at a kitchen island nearby, putting the finishing touches on a salad.

"It smells good," she said. "Like that Indian restaurant on Dupont Circle."

"Chicken marsala. It's supposed to smell like that."

"I'm sorry I had to do that today," Selena said. "I didn't want to humiliate him. He was getting angry. When people get angry they make mistakes. I thought it was time to stop it before one of us got hurt."

"You did the right thing. He's young and he still has a lot to learn."

"He's twenty-seven."

"Like I said, he's young. He hasn't learned how to hold his anger in check when things are going against him. That's not a good trait."

"I like him though," Selena said. "He showed respect, once he could stand."

"I saw that. I think he heard what I said when I told him he could learn from you."

"He did well on the range."

"After years in the Rangers he ought to," Nick said. "He showed good judgment on the combat course. He only shot one civilian. That's better than I did the first time through."

The urban combat course was recent, installed in the large warehouse across from Headquarters. It consisted of movable walls and props that looked like the streets and buildings of an urban environment anywhere in the world. It could be configured as a village street, a city block or a mockup of a mission target, depending on need. Three-dimensional automated targets popped out in unpredictable ways from doors and windows, inside rooms and from behind walls and vehicles. Some were enemies, with a variety of weapons and looks. Others were civilians: old men, office workers, children, women with babies. Ramirez had shot one of the old men, thinking his cane was a gun. Grading depended on hits, accurate identification of the target and speed of response.

Selena said, "He's getting into it. I can see him trying to figure it out. He still doesn't know what we do, not really."

"He won't, until he's in the field."

Nick checked the chicken. "It's done."

"You realize this is our first real dinner here?" Selena said.

"Won't be the last," Nick said.

"You're a real romantic, aren't you?"

Here was a remodeled loft looking out over the Potomac. They'd moved in a few days before. They'd bought it together even though they weren't married. Nick figured they would be. In the meantime, the loft was a way to commit to each other before getting to the altar. So far they hadn't set a date or made arrangements for the final step.

"What do you think about our rookie?" Selena asked. "Do you think he's going to fit?"

"He looks pretty good," Nick said. "I think the biggest problem is going to be whether or not he can let go of his self-image."

"His self-image?"

"Macho Ranger, superhero."

"Oh, that image."

"Army Rangers are like that."

"Do I hear the Marine Corps Hymn playing in the background?" Selena said.

"What do you mean?"

"You know what I mean. That Marine thing about other units."

"The Rangers are a good unit."

"Are they as good as the Marines?"

"Marines are the best," Nick said, "but the Rangers are damn good."

"I rest my case," Selena said.

CHAPTER 6

Nazar Al-Bayati sported a heavy brush of a mustache like the one worn by Saddam Hussein. He was heavy, thick around the waist. His arms were the size of many men's thighs. He had once crushed a man to death with those arms to make a point.

Some made their money selling guns or drugs or women. Nazar sold all of those, but his main source of income was information. He lived at the center of a web of thieves and spies that reached across the Middle East and Europe, from the back alleys of Damascus to the corporate board rooms of London and Paris.

Not much of importance in the Middle East escaped his notice. For Al-Bayati, the endless wars were a blessing from God. Not that he believed in God. He believed in an insatiable deity of a darker nature, worshipped by his Carthaginian ancestors in centuries past. Nazar's god was old, older than the one revered by Christian, Jew and Muslim alike. It was to him that he directed his prayers and supplications.

The only other thing he believed in was greed. An intelligent and cunning man, Nazar found his most profitable information came from new developments in technology. New weapons, new discoveries, better ways to wage war. All these things equaled new ways to make money. The man who knew what was coming would always stay one step ahead of his competitors. To that end he had informers watching for information he could turn into profit. He had eyes in the nuclear facilities of Russia, men who watched the Israelis, and men in the temples of science in Europe. It was one of these who had told him about the odd looking Italian and his volcanic scroll. Nazar had dispatched his agent at once.

Professor Caprini's overnight bag rested on the desk in front of him. Nazar looked up at the man who had brought it. His name was Addison Rhoades, a disgraced British spy who'd become one of Bayati's most valuable assets. Rhoades was Bayati's fixer, the man who took care of problems. A small problem, Rhoades took care of it himself. A large one, he knew men who could do what needed to be done.

At first glance Rhoades looked like a successful European businessman. He was dressed in a good suit, a light blue shirt and a lavender tie knotted to perfection. A closer inspection revealed the dissipation in his face, the tight lines around his eyes and the darkness under them. He was tall, stronger than he looked and a highly trained assassin.

"You opened the bag?" Nazar said.

"Yes. The scroll lies in a case within."

"Are there notes?"

"There's a computer. I haven't looked at it but if there are notes, that's where they'll be. There are copies of the x-rays."

"Excellent. I assume you left no traces behind."

"You haven't read the papers today?"

Nazar thought. "The train in Italy?"

"Yes."

"Ah. A bit extreme, wasn't it?"

"It seemed best," Rhoades said.

"Who else knows about the x-rays?" Nazar asked.

"As far as I know, only one person. The technician who operated the machine."

"I want you to go back to Grenoble," Nazar said. "Eliminate him. Destroy any records of the results as well."

"That may involve damage to some very expensive equipment," Rhoades said.

"It's of no importance. The French will repair it. Make it look like some kind of terrorist attack."

"As you wish."

"You've done well, Addison."

Nazar reached into a drawer. He took out a small, foil wrapped ball. Rhoades wet his lips. Nazar saw the longing on his face.

"Make sure this doesn't interfere with your mission."

"Of course," Rhoades said. He took the ball, placing it in his pocket.

When Rhoades had left, Nazar opened Professor Caprini's laptop and booted it up. The screen requested a password. Nazar inserted a flash drive loaded with a program stolen from Russian intelligence. The screen went dark for a moment then cleared, revealing a dozen file folders against a blue background. Nazar clicked on the one marked Herculaneum.

The file contained the pictures taken in Grenoble, showing what lay beneath the crusted surface of the scroll. Even crystal x-ray tomography wasn't good enough to show what was written on most of the ancient document. But what had been revealed was enough to set Nazar's black heart beating.

CHAPTER 7

Stephanie and Elizabeth were in Elizabeth's office when Nick and Selena arrived. Ronnie came in right after them.

"I got a heads-up from the White House," Elizabeth said. "Rice wants us to look into something that happened in France."

"If there's a chance we're going out soon you'd better get Ramirez in here," Nick said. "He needs to be in on the planning."

"Have you decided to keep him?"

"I don't know yet but this seems like a good time to show him how we work."

"Last I saw of our rookie, he was in the workout room. Steph, would you ask Sergeant Ramirez to come up here please?"

Down in the workout room Diego was on the treadmill, running in place. His mind was going faster than his feet.

Who the hell are these people? he thought. *This is one weird set up. Hell, they're old, Carter and his Indian buddy. I wonder what happened to his ear? The blonde, Selena. Where did she learn to fight like that? And the whole operation is being run by a woman.*

He punched a button. The speed picked up.

Those weapons in the armory...they're not fooling around. I still don't know what it is they do. If they're not spooks, what are they? Problem solvers, Harker said. What the hell does that mean? What kind of problems?

Stephanie came to the door. "Sergeant, Director Harker wants you upstairs."

"Right away."

He shut down the machine, felt his body thinking his feet were still moving. Stephanie was already gone. Diego mopped his brow with a towel and went upstairs.

Once Ramirez was seated, Harker got to the point.

"Sergeant, you are still on probation but Nick and I thought you should be here to see how we approach an operation. Put up the pictures please, Steph."

Stephanie touched a key on her laptop. The monitor on Elizabeth's office wall sprang to life with a picture of a large, gray building that looked like a giant doughnut. The walls and roof were one, rounded unit. The structure made a full circle, with a large open area in the center. Blackened, twisted metal showed where the force of an explosion had blown a large hole in the side.

"Looks like somebody took a bite out of it," Ronnie said.

He was wearing a faded blue Hawaiian shirt from his collection, covered with happy ukulele players strumming their instruments and wearing leis.

"Speaking of looks, you look like a music hall in old Waikiki," Nick said. "Where did you get that shirt? The Goodwill store?"

"Hey, this is a classic from the 70s. When are you going to learn to appreciate the finer points of being well-dressed?"

"Excuse me," Elizabeth said, "I wonder if I could have your attention?"

"Sorry, Director," Nick said

Ramirez watched the exchange in disbelief.

"What is that place in the picture?" Nick asked.

"The European Synchrotron Radiation Facility in Grenoble, France."

"That's a mouthful."

"It's one of the world's top facilities for studying x-rays and radiation, not to mention physics and chemistry. It's a very big deal. Someone just put it out of commission, as you can see."

"Terrorist attack?" Selena asked.

"That's the official line."

"What's the unofficial?"

"Unofficially, no one knows anything except that it was sabotage. The area that was targeted deals with a specialized technique called crystal x-ray tomography. It's like a super CAT scan, only instead of people it scans objects. The files and equipment in that part of the building were destroyed. Selena, you can read Aramaic. Is that right?"

"It depends. Usually I can."

"It's routine for all files created at the facility to be duplicated on another server. The research is too important to trust to only one backup source. The explosion destroyed one server but the files still exist on the backup. French security found x-rays of a scroll written in Aramaic taken in the days just before the attack."

"That's interesting, but how does it relate to the explosion?"

"The scroll could be the reason for it. It was sealed in volcanic debris during the eruption of Vesuvius. A professor from the Italian National Museum named Caprini brought it in to see if the text could be read by using x-rays. It turned out that the first page and part of the second could be seen. Caprini was a biblical archaeologist. He knew how to translate it."

"Was a biblical archaeologist?"

"He's dead. That's one reason the French think the scroll has something to do with this. He was headed back to Italy when an explosion blew him and his train off a bridge in the Italian Alps. It wasn't an accident."

"I read about that," Ronnie said. "More than two hundred people died in that wreck."

Nick looked at Harker. "You said one reason. There are others?"

"The technician who operated the x-ray equipment for Caprini was found dead after the explosion. He was killed before the blast."

"Someone murdered him?" Selena asked.

"Yes."

"Where's the scroll?"

"Good question. Caprini had the scroll and copies of the x-ray results with him on the train. No trace of them was found in the wreck."

"Was the facility attacked before or after the train wreck?" Nick asked.

"The day after."

"Seems like a big coincidence, two explosions involving that scroll."

"I don't believe in coincidences. Neither does French security. While he was in Grenoble, Caprini let it slip that the scroll could start a new war in the Middle East."

"I'm getting really tired of going to the Middle East," Nick said. "The damn place is always full of people killing each other in the name of God."

"You may be going there again. It depends on what's on that scroll and why someone would want to kill for it. The French think the explosion at the facility was an attempt to destroy records of what the x-rays revealed. They also think there's a connection with the attack on the train."

"How did you find that out?" Nick asked.

"I have a contact in DGSE, French security. The French government doesn't always cooperate with us but in this case my contact thought he should give me a heads-up. Anything that could light off the Middle East concerns both Paris and Washington. I thought the president ought to know about it. He told me to follow up. Steph, can we see the next picture?"

The x-rays of the scroll appeared on the monitor. Selena leaned forward to get a better look. There were few people in the world as knowledgeable as her when it came to understanding the ancient languages of the Middle East.

The pictures showed ghostly images of white writing against a black background. They looked like rows of chicken tracks. There were gaps in the writing. A faint second layer could be seen underneath the first, a different part of the rolled scroll. The letters were difficult to see, the lines of writing incomplete.

Selena studied the pictures. "This is Aramaic from around the time of the Roman conquest of Judea. It was very common then. Everyone used it."

"When was that?" Ronnie asked.

"The Romans conquered Jerusalem in 63 CE."

Before she'd joined the Project Selena had been in high demand on the university circuit, lecturing on the dead languages of the ancient world. For Selena, reading Aramaic was like reading an out of date newspaper.

"Can you read it?" Elizabeth asked.

"Yes, but I'll need to consult some references."

"Can you have something for me by morning?"
"Make a copy and I'll take it home with me."

CHAPTER 8

"This is going to upset a lot of people," Selena said.

It was later that night. Open books and pieces of paper with scribbled notes littered the surface of the table in front of her. Nick looked up from a book about a sheriff in Wyoming who was shadowed by the ghosts of dead warriors. He was someone Nick could relate to.

"Can you read the scroll?"

"The part that was x-rayed. It's too bad it can't be unrolled. No one will ever see the rest of it but what there is will make a lot of trouble."

"What does it say?"

"It's an account by a man named Ephram. He seems to have been part of the Jewish resistance to Roman rule that brought on the first Jewish-Roman war, back in 66 CE. That's four years before the Romans crushed the revolt and destroyed the Second Temple."

"Please don't tell me this is going to get everyone upset about the Temple."

"It will, and it's not just the Temple. This mentions one of the most famous people in the Bible, King Solomon."

"I thought that was just a story," Nick said. "About Solomon. Like in the book *King Solomon's Mines.* The Queen of Sheba, lost treasures, all that."

"Many historians believe Sheba and Solomon were real," Selena said. "No one's quite sure where Solomon's kingdom was. It was probably Israel and part of what's now Jordan and Egypt. According to the Bible, King David was his father. The scroll says Solomon was buried near David, in a place called Ir. That's the City of David in modern-day Jerusalem and the scroll seems to verify the biblical story. By itself it's enough to get everybody excited."

"If Solomon was buried in Jerusalem, how come nobody has dug him up?"

"Because he's not there anymore. The scroll says his bones were taken away as the Romans advanced on Jerusalem. That's not all. The sacred objects of the Temple went with him, a treasure that would be priceless today. The Jews were afraid the Romans would desecrate the tomb and violate the Temple. I don't know about the tomb but they destroyed the Temple after they looted it. "

"Does the scroll say where everything was taken?"

"South to the mountains of Edom and the kingdom of the Dedanites."

"I never heard of Edom or the Dedanites."

"The kingdom of Dedan was in what's now Saudi Arabia, between the desert and the coast of the Red Sea. It's desolate country. There's nothing there but sand, rock and a few villages built high in the mountains."

"Sounds like a perfect place to hide something," Nick said.

"Ephram writes that everything was placed in a hidden tomb. When this gets out, everyone will start looking for it."

"You think it will get out?"

"Of course it will. Too many people already know about it for it to stay secret for very long."

"I see what you mean about it causing trouble," Nick said. "The Israelis would do anything to recover something from the Temple. It's going to get political."

"You can count on it. The zealots will have a field day. The Arabs want to deny Israel any claim on Jerusalem or the Temple Mount. Anything from the Temple would strengthen the Jewish claim, not to mention the remains of Solomon. If everything is in Saudi Arabia, that really complicates things."

"If we know about the scroll so do the Israelis," Nick said. "Israeli intelligence is good. Mossad will have copies of the x-rays by now. They'll be reading the same thing you are. The Arabs won't take it well if the Israelis start snooping around on their turf."

"That's putting it mildly." Selena pushed aside her notes and massaged her forehead. "It gives me a headache, thinking about it. Do you think whoever blew up the train set off the explosion in Grenoble?"

Nick rubbed the stubble on his chin. "Yeah, I do. It's too much of a coincidence. The Israelis could have done it but I don't think it was them. Taking out the train is overkill, they wouldn't need to do that. It's not their style. It could be someone we don't know about, a third-party with an interest in finding the treasure."

"It's not going to be easy to do that even if it still exists," Selena said.

"Is there anything you read that gives something specific about location?"

"There's a section I can't translate yet. There may be something on the next page but it's difficult to read. There are large gaps and what I can see is faint, much less defined."

"Sounds like something Stephanie could help with," Nick said. "There must be some historical mention of what happened to the Temple treasure."

"The only thing I've ever seen is speculation that it was hidden in caves underneath the Temple and later stolen. Or perhaps found by the Templars. Nobody knows," Selena said.

"Okay. But if there is something else, Steph will find it."

Selena yawned. She looked at the clock over the stove.

"My brain is fried." She stretched and yawned again. "I'm tired."

"Let's go to bed," Nick said.

"I'm looking forward to some sleep."

"Just sleep?" He put his arms around her.

"You have a better idea?"

"You know I do," he said.

She reached up and ran her hand over the side of his face. Her fingers touched the scar where a bullet had taken off part of his left ear. His cheek was rough with stubble. She looked into his eyes, gray with hints of gold.

"Why don't you show me what you have in mind?" she said.

CHAPTER 9

DCI Clarence Hood shook hands with his new Director of Clandestine Operations.

"Congratulations, Lucas."

The official Langley photographer snapped a few quick pictures. It wasn't every day that one of the four major directorates at Langley got a new boss. The DCO oversaw all of the secretive operations carried out by Langley's vast intelligence apparatus.

At first glance there was nothing in particular about Lucas Monroe to draw attention. He was of medium height, with skin the color of dark chocolate. It was his eyes that hinted at something best left undisturbed. There were hard lines around them, as if they'd seen more than they wanted to. He wore a gray jacket and dark slacks. The jacket concealed a pistol in a shoulder holster under his left arm.

It was an old habit to keep it with him, even though he no longer had as much need for it. Lucas had been a field agent for years, his exploits already the stuff of legend at Langley. He'd earned his new job the hard way, with smart decisions and a large helping of balls. He was the first black man to hold down one of the major directorates.

"That will do it, Clark."

"Yes, sir." The photographer left the room.

Hood gestured at a pair of leather armchairs in the corner of his office.

"Care for a drink? You've earned it. Come to think of it, so have I."

Hood's voice was mellow, touched with the soft accent of his southern birth. He was a tall man, almost cadaverous. The bones of his face stood out under pale skin lined with more than thirty years of service as a spy. He'd been appointed Director of Central Intelligence by President Rice after the apparent suicide of his predecessor.

"This is a special cask reserve from Kentucky," Hood said. "Best damn bourbon I ever had."

Hood poured two generous shots from a cut crystal decanter and handed one to Lucas.

"Confusion to our enemies," Hood said. They drank.

The two men sat down. Hood's office took up one corner of the seventh floor in the old headquarters building. From where they sat, they could look out over the rolling hills of Virginia, where the remnants of Lee's Army of Northern Virginia had retreated before Grant's forces in the final days of the Civil War.

"You're starting with a full plate," Hood said.

"It's always a full plate. At least it has been as long as I've been here."

"Now that you're DCO, you'll find there are some who resent your promotion. Some because they're jealous, some because of the color of your skin."

"That won't be anything new," Lucas said. "Thanks for the heads-up. I can handle it."

"I know that. One thing you've got going for you is your reputation as an agent. The experienced operatives respect that and they'll respect you. The problems are going to come from people who haven't been through the fire like you have. I'm not telling you anything you don't already know."

"I can handle it," Lucas said again. He changed the subject. "There are several ongoing operations I've been tracking. I don't see any immediate problems. I'm more concerned with new developments, especially that scroll that turned up in France."

"Yes, that could be a problem." Hood sipped his drink.

"I'm making it a priority," Lucas said. "I've seen the x-rays and translation. The word is spreading fast. If what's on that scroll is true, it could trigger a war over there. The Israelis, the Saudis and every cutthroat in the Middle East will be after that treasure. It's bound to lead to confrontations. We need to find out who took it. I have a lead but I need more information."

"You've identified who is behind it?" Hood asked.

"We traced the chemical signature of the Semtex used to blow up the train. It came from a lot that went missing during the Bosnian war. We tracked that to a black-market arms dealer in Lebanon. I think we should have a conversation with him."

"What do you intend to do?"

"That's something I want to talk to you about. I'm concerned about leaks. Someone here has been talking to the media when they shouldn't. The last thing we need is the press thinking we have anything to do with that train wreck. I have an idea that might bypass that particular problem."

"Yes?"

"I'd like to use Harker's group, instead of our people. Until I can find and plug the leak, I want to keep this under wraps."

Hood raised an eyebrow. "I can see how it might be an advantage to take it out of house but you're engaged to Harker's deputy. You don't think it's a conflict of interest?"

"Stephanie's clearance is as high as mine. She understands the game. It's not like I'm going to be telling her or Harker what to do. That wouldn't work out well."

Hood laughed. "No, I don't think it would. Harker doesn't like people telling her what to do."

"Neither does Stephanie. We'll need the president's authorization to do it that way. You're on good terms with him. I thought I'd talk to Harker and perhaps you could handle the White House."

"Now I see why you're the right choice for the job," Hood said.

CHAPTER 10

Diego Ramirez was lying down reading a magazine. Nick came to his open door.

"You like Chinese, Diego?"

"I don't know any Chinese."

"I meant food, not people. Come on, Sergeant, we're all going out to eat and you're invited."

"I never turn down food," Diego said. "What's the occasion?"

"Stephanie is engaged. This is a kind of late celebration. There's a great Chinese restaurant in Alexandria we like to go to once in a while. You'll get to meet her fiancé, Lucas Munroe. He's CIA."

"CIA?"

Nick heard unspoken judgment in Diego's voice.

"He's good people. Five minutes," Nick said. He turned and went back upstairs.

Ramirez shook his head. *CIA. It figures.*

Ronnie was waiting for them outside with his black Hummer.

"The women went ahead in Harker's car," Ronnie said. "Hop in."

Diego climbed in back. "Nice wheels."

Ronnie pulled away. "I've modified it some," he said. "It's not exactly stock anymore. Armor and more horsepower. See that lid on the floor in back of you?"

Ramirez turned and looked. "Yeah?"

A numbered keypad was set into the lid.

"Punch in 1-7-7-6. Lift up that handle and take a look."

Ramirez leaned over the seat, entered the code and lifted the lid. Four MP-5s, a dozen loaded magazines, flash bangs and a Remington 870 12 gauge lay inside the compartment.

"Holy shit," he said. "You've got a whole arsenal in here."

"I like to be prepared."

"What, you were in the Boy Scouts?"

"I figured you ought to know about it. It's come in handy before."

Ramirez let the lid down and turned back to face the front.

"This is Virginia. You need that stuff here?"

"Purely defensive," Ronnie said.

Nick laughed. "In case you haven't figured it out yet, Diego, the bad guys don't like us much. They don't care if we're in Virginia."

Nobody had anything to say the rest of the way into town. Ronnie parked half a block from the restaurant.

The Happy Family restaurant was set back from the street at the end of a short sidewalk flanked by two dragons cast in bronze. The three men walked toward an elaborate pagoda-style entrance painted green and red. Odors of Chinese cooking filled the evening air.

"Smells good," Nick said.

Across the street, a dog began yelping in pain. They looked over. A large man was beating a beagle with a stick. The dog cowered against the pavement and began howling.

"Hey!" Ramirez shouted. "Cut that shit out."

The man turned and looked at him.

"Mind your own business," he said. He raised the stick and hit the dog again.

Ramirez ran across the street and grabbed the man's arm before he could bring the stick down another time. He twisted the arm and sent the stick flying. The dog whimpered and shivered on the sidewalk.

"Want to try picking on someone who can hit back?" Diego said.

The man smelled of beer and cigarettes. He was a large man. Diego looked small beside him.

"You just made a big mistake, buddy."

The dog beater launched a roundhouse right with a ham-sized fist. Diego blocked it with ease and snapped a quick, hard right into the man's face with the flattened palm of his hand. He felt the nose break. Blood poured out. The man howled in pain and grabbed Diego in a bear hug. Ramirez leaned back and head butted him, hard.

They could hear the impact across the street.

Nick winced. "Oooh."

"That had to hurt," Ronnie said. "Our boy has a temper."

The dog beater went to his knees, holding his hands to his face. Farther down the sidewalk, an elderly couple stopped and stared at the scene.

"Game over," Nick said.

Diego reached down and fished out the man's wallet. He looked at the driver's license. Then he tossed the wallet on the ground.

"Now I know who you are and where you live," he said. "I'm going to check up on you. I'm going to watch and see how your dog is doing. If you touch him again, I'm going to give you a beating that will make today look like an invitation to the junior prom. *Comprende, pendejo?* Understand?"

"Yes, yes. Don't hit me again."

The dog looked up at Diego. His tail thumped twice against the sidewalk.

"Good boy. It's okay, he won't do that again. Will you, asshole?"

"No."

"Then we're done."

He walked back across the street to where the others waited.

"Asshole," he muttered under his breath.

"We better go inside," Ronnie said.

"I hate people who abuse animals. I see it, I have to do something about it. It's been that way ever since I was a kid. Got me in trouble sometimes."

"How's your head?" Nick asked.

"Better than his. I got a head like a rock."

Stephanie, Selena and Elizabeth were seated at a large round table set apart from the others in the restaurant. Lucas Munroe sat next to Stephanie.

"Lucas, this is Diego Ramirez. He might take Lamont's spot on the team."

The two men shook hands. Nick, Diego and Ronnie sat down.

"Congratulations on your promotion, Lucas," Elizabeth said.

"Thank you."

"Way to go," Nick said. "You deserve it."

"Diego, you've got blood on your shirt," Selena said.

"It's nothing. It's not mine."

"What happened, Nick?" Elizabeth asked. "We heard a dog howling."

"Sergeant Ramirez had to give a little lesson in animal ethics to a man who thought his dog needed beating."

"Oh, one of them," Stephanie said. "Some people should never be allowed to have an animal."

"I think he learned his lesson," Ronnie said.

A waiter took their orders.

"The drunken chicken is good here," Lucas said.

"I always wondered why they call it that," Selena said. "I get this picture in my mind of a bunch of chickens staggering around the barnyard."

"Probably had more to do with the cook who invented it," Nick said.

There was a brief pause.

"I hear you're looking into what happened in France," Lucas said.

Elizabeth looked at Stephanie.

"It wasn't me," she said. "Lucas brought it up. I didn't tell him anything."

"We have some interest, yes," Elizabeth said.

"So do we." He looked at Diego. "I assume he's fully vetted?"

Elizabeth nodded. "You can speak freely."

Lucas picked up a set of chopsticks in a paper wrapper, took them out and broke them apart. He set them down again on the table.

"That scroll could cause a lot of grief."

"Have you read it?" Selena asked.

Lucas nodded. "I read a translation. We think the professor who brought it to Grenoble was murdered because of it. The bomb in his train compartment was Semtex, more than was needed to kill him. Someone wanted to wipe out any evidence that might lead back to them."

"Who put it there?" Nick asked.

"That's the question. We traced the chemical signature. The Semtex came from an arms shipment stolen in Serbia right after the Bosnian war. Some of the weapons turned up in Africa not too long ago."

"Any idea who was behind the theft?" Elizabeth asked.

"We're not sure," Lucas said. "We think it was a Lebanese arms dealer named Yusuf Abidi."

"That doesn't mean he's the one who planted the bomb," Elizabeth said.

"No, it doesn't. We traced the weapons in Africa back to him. It's likely that at some point the Semtex was in his possession. If it wasn't him, he might know who it was."

"Where does this guy hang out?" Ronnie asked.

"Beirut."

"Are you going after him?" Selena asked.

Lucas smiled. "No, you are. Hey, here comes the food."

Conversation was minimal while they dug into the steaming platters.

After they'd eaten, the waiter cleared away the debris. He left a check and a plate of fortune cookies.

"Cool," Diego said. "Fortune cookies."

They all took one. Diego cracked his open and pulled out the piece of paper inside.

"Beware the Ides of March," he said. "That's original."

"Good thing your name isn't Caesar," Lucas said.

Selena read hers to them. "A handsome man is in your future."

"Hey," Nick said.

"Don't blame me. Can I help it if fate has something in store?"

"What's yours, Nick?" Elizabeth asked.

"You'll soon discover the truth about the one you love." He looked at Selena. "Is there something you want to tell me? About a handsome man, maybe?"

Ronnie opened his. "Mine says I will live long. That's good to know."

"These cookies suck," Diego said.

"What did you expect, the wisdom of the ages?"

"Well, yeah. You know, Confucius and all that."

Selena looked at Lucas. "It sounds like our future is already planned out. What did you mean about us going after him?"

"Langley is like a Libyan freighter these days. There are too many leaks. I talked it over with Hood. We thought your group would be able to keep things quiet. If word got out that the CIA was looking into that train wreck the media would be on it like white on rice."

"What have you got on this Lebanese arms dealer?" Nick asked.

"He's tight with Hezbollah and they provide protection for him. They're one of his best customers. He's careful to keep them happy."

"I thought Hezbollah had been brought under control by the Lebanese, except on the border with Israel," Selena said.

Lucas laughed. "Sure they have."

"What did you have in mind?" Elizabeth said.

She sounded annoyed. Acting in place of Langley wasn't part of her job description. Lucas picked up on it.

"Look, we're not asking you to do more than find out what you can from Abidi. Hood has already talked with the president."

"Why do you need us?"

"There's been too much negative publicity about Langley in the last few years. We're everybody's favorite villain as far as the press is concerned. We have a leak and until I find out who's talking to them I want to keep a low profile."

Elizabeth understood about keeping a low profile. There were powerful people with their own agendas who didn't understand what was required to keep the country safe. They wanted all the comforts security brought without any of the responsibility for the uncomfortable decisions that made security possible. Accountability was one thing. Politically correct witch hunts were another. Sometimes the two became confused.

"You should have discussed this with me before going to the president."

"I'm sorry," Lucas said. "You're right. It won't happen again."

"Tell Director Hood I'm going to be speaking with him," Elizabeth said.

I'd like to hear that conversation, Nick thought.

"Then you're on board?"

"I work for the president. If this is what he wants, of course I am."

Stephanie gave Lucas an accusing glance. "You set this up."

"I figured you needed something to do."

"I have plenty to do."

"You want to tell them?"

"Tell us what?" Elizabeth said.

Selena saw Lucas take Stephanie's hand. He had a foolish smile on his face.

Stephanie looked radiant. "We're going to have a baby."

Elizabeth's response took a second or two. "Steph, that's wonderful."

Nick said, "Congratulations, Lucas."

"When are you due, Steph?" Selena said.

"A little over five months from now."

"Is it a boy or a girl?"

"We don't know yet."

Elizabeth looked at her deputy. The pregnancy would complicate things. She'd come to rely on Steph's ability to coax information from the computers and the surveillance satellites that circled the globe. Stephanie managed the complicated communications network that kept Elizabeth in touch with the team in the field. Without her, even for a short time, everything would become more complicated. The baby would change everything.

I wonder how long she'll keep working? I'd better start thinking about finding someone to back her up, Elizabeth thought.

Later Nick and Selena drove back to the city.

Selena said, "Steph looks wonderful, don't you think?"

"Mm," Nick said.

"And Lucas. That hard, tough man, all warm and cuddly."

"Cuddly is not a word I would use to describe Lucas."

"You know what I mean."

"It's going to make things difficult," Nick said.

"Why do you say that? People have babies all the time."

"Most people aren't computer geniuses who happen to be an indispensable part of an intelligence unit."

Selena's voice took on a hint of coolness. "I'm sure she'll work right up until the time she gives birth. It shouldn't make any difference at all."

"What about after? What about when she has to take care of a baby? What if the baby gets sick? All of that is going to affect how she's able to work and the quality of what she does."

"Why do men always assume that having a baby is going to make the woman into some kind of an idiot? Someone who can't work up to her ability?"

"I didn't say that."

"That's what you meant."

"That's not what I meant."

"I don't think we should talk about this anymore," Selena said. She turned away and looked out the window.

The rest of the ride to town was spent in silence.

CHAPTER 11

Elizabeth talked with DCI Hood. Then she talked with the president. Two days later the team and Diego flew into Rafik Hariri International Airport in Beirut. In the back of the Gulfstream was an aluminum case with their pistols. They hadn't brought anything heavy with them. Their diplomatic passports in false names got them through customs without incident. They took rooms in a modern hotel in the heart of the city.

Beirut was effectively divided into three zones, controlled by the different sectarian groups that kept the city and the country fragmented. The Sunni Muslims held the western part, the Christians the east. The Shia Muslims lived in the southern section, run by Iran's proxy Hezbollah. The difference between the three sections was enormous. Where the Sunnis and the Christians were in charge Beirut functioned much as other cities did, with more or less adequate services and a reasonable expectation of order and personal safety. Of course safety was relative. A lot depended on who you were and on which religion you belonged to.

In the west and the east of the city people were mostly tolerant of each other, regardless of religion. In the south where Hezbollah held power, tolerance was not a word anyone used or understood. Southern Beirut was an entity unto itself. The government stayed away from the area and left the fanatical militant group alone. Nobody wanted another internal war no one could win.

Lebanon's civil war had destroyed large parts of what had once been a beautiful, cosmopolitan city. Parts of downtown had been restored in an effort to preserve what was left of the Parisian style French architecture, and attempt to reassure a slowly reviving tourist trade that all was well. The effect was something that would have seemed at home on the Strip in Las Vegas. The streets were clean and reasonably modern. The garbage was collected. The streetlights worked. That was more than could be said for the area south of the unofficial dividing line.

Yusuf Abidi lived in the southern part of the city, on the top floor of a crumbling twelve story building. The bottom two floors were leased out to a charitable organization that formed a front for Hezbolla. It provided a convenient conduit for some of Abidi's shipments. Hezbolla was one of his best customers.

Small arms, ammunition, explosives, heavy machine guns, Russian rocket launchers and the like were the staples of Yusuf's trade. From time to time, he negotiated larger deals for older models of Russian tanks, armored vehicles, antiaircraft batteries and heavy weapons, along with the occasional French fighter jet or two. Authentic end-user certificates purchased with large bribes protected the more obvious transactions.

Most of the large items went to Africa, where regional warlords and dictators happily blew each other's people to pieces with Abidi's products. They had an insatiable appetite for AKs, of which there was an endless supply. The bread-and-butter of his business was the daily hardware of death in the Middle East. For Abidi, the rise of ISIS had been a gift from Allah.

Business was booming. All in all, Abidi was a happy man. He wouldn't have been as happy if he'd known he was being watched.

On the third day after they'd arrived Nick, Ronnie, Diego and Selena sat in a black Mercedes with tinted windows, watching the entrance to Abidi's building. The street in front of the building was narrow, in poor repair. Several seedy looking Hezbollah fighters lounged in front, their AKs openly displayed. The façade of the building was pockmarked where bullets had struck it sometime in the past. The architecture was completely forgettable. The building looked solid, unlike most of the others on the block. Under Hezbollah control southern Beirut was a sprawling slum. The entire block looked like a perfect candidate for urban renewal. Nick kept the windows rolled up and the air conditioner on against the heat and the clinging stench coming from piles of uncollected garbage lining the curbs.

Selena wore a full head scarf and a shapeless dress that concealed her regular clothes and reached to her ankles. Long sleeves covered her arms even in the heat of the Lebanese summer. Her conservative Muslim look blended in. She would draw little attention. The dress was hot. At least it had the advantage of hiding her pistol.

The men wore casual clothes indistinguishable from the locals. Nick's tan and a three-day stubble concealed some of his foreignness. At a quick glance, Diego and Ronnie could pass for being from somewhere in the Middle East. The tinted windows of the Mercedes made it difficult for anyone to see in.

The plan was to isolate Abidi and question him. They were still in observational mode. They had to wait for the right opportunity. So far it hadn't occurred. Everyone on the team wore transceivers that allowed them to communicate with each other and by satellite link with Elizabeth and Stephanie back in Virginia

"I don't understand why talking to this guy is such a big deal," Diego said.

"You're not supposed to understand." It was Ronnie. "It's beyond your pay grade."

"Yeah? But not beyond yours?"

"It's a big deal because the president is concerned," Nick said. "He has to know if the treasure is real or not. It's potentially real trouble. Temple relics would strengthen the Jewish claim on the Temple Mount."

"So?"

"Anything that validates Israeli control of Jerusalem is like a time bomb. If it goes off, it will take the Middle East with it. If we can find out who Abidi sold that Semtex to, we'll know who has the scroll. Then we can figure out what comes next."

In Virginia, Elizabeth and Stephanie were monitoring a live shot from a drone circling high above Abidi's building and the car where the team waited. Elizabeth spoke into her headset.

"Abidi should be leaving any time now."

"Copy," Nick answered.

Their target usually left the security of his building at about eleven in the morning for his office in a warehouse near the port. He would stay there until three or four in the afternoon. After that, his movements were unpredictable until he returned to his apartment some time in the evening.

As they watched the building a new, white BMW 760i pulled up to the entrance. The driver sat in the car while two bodyguards emerged, carrying submachine pistols. They were large men, unsmiling. They looked up and down the street. They saw the Mercedes and passed over it.

"Skorpion vz61s," Nick said. "Nasty."

"Old and efficient," Ronnie said.

Diego nodded at the car. "That beemer's top-of-the-line. Twelve cylinders, over five hundred horses."

"My kind of car," Selena said.

"There he is," Nick said.

Abidi came out of the building. He wore a light beige suit and dark glasses. He was an unimposing man, with black hair and an olive tinted complexion. His shoes gleamed in the sunlight. One of the guards held the rear door open until Abidi had gotten into the car. The bodyguard closed the door, walked around to the other side and got in. The second guard got into the front. The car pulled away, headed for the harbor. Nick pulled out after him.

"Target acquired, moving," Nick said.

"Copy that," Elizabeth answered. "We see you."

They followed the BMW through heavy traffic. The white car continued past the point where Abidi normally turned off toward his warehouse. It kept going, headed south.

The shabby high rise buildings of the city gave way to flat roofed slums two and three stories high. The street was potholed, dirty. Emaciated dogs lay unmoving in the sun or rooted in piles of trash by the side of the road. Bearded men carrying rifles seemed to be everywhere, watching the Mercedes go by with suspicious eyes.

The flag of Hezbollah flew from almost every building, a stylized assault rifle in green against a bright yellow background. Red and green letters in Arabic completed the design.

"Hezbollah country," Nick said. "I don't like this. If something happens we're outgunned."

"What does the Arabic on the flag say?" Ronnie asked.

Selena said, "The main logo under the rifle says Party of God. The rest of it says they'll be victorious and that they are the resistance in Lebanon."

"Yeah, right," Diego said. "Resistance to what? They're the main reason this country is so screwed up."

"Where's Abidi going?" Ronnie watched the white BMW ahead.

Traffic was light along the highway. Nick dropped back. It was easy to see the distinctive white car.

"How would I know? Maybe it will give us an opportunity to grab him. Director, are you following?"

"Affirmative, Nick. Stay back and don't engage. Let's see what he's up to."

"Copy."

On the open highway the big BMW carrying Abidi picked up speed. The Mercedes was a rental, older. Nick hoped it was up to the task. It was 104° outside. He kept a wary eye on the temperature gauge. Off to their right, the blue Mediterranean swept by, the kind of view tourists died for. In Lebanon, dying for a view could turn out to be more than just a phrase.

They had only gone a few miles from the city when they entered another stretch of slums. The BMW slowed before turning in toward a walled compound. The car pulled up in front of a massive iron gate set in a high wall. Beyond, Nick glimpsed a large villa. He continued past for another mile until he was out of the built up area and pulled over to the side of the road.

"Director, can you get any info on that villa?"

"Not yet. Wait one."

In Virginia Elizabeth said, "Steph, focus on that building."

Stephanie touched her keyboard. The drone camera zoomed in on the compound.

"Nick," Elizabeth said, "I don't know who's in there but it looks like it's heavily fortified. There's a guardhouse. Two men patrolling. Razor wire on the walls."

"Who owns it?"

"I'm on it," Stephanie said.

She entered a string of commands, using the drone to pin down the location and from there a specific address. That led to a string of documents.

"I've got records. They're in Arabic."

"Send them to Selena," Elizabeth said. "Selena, I'm sending you something for translation."

Stephanie pressed a key. In Lebanon, Selena's phone played *Love Me Tender.*

"Elvis?" Ronnie said.

"I like him."

"Retro," Diego said. "I would've figured you for something a little newer."

"I don't care much for modern music," Selena said. "With Elvis I can understand what he's singing about."

Diego rolled his eyes.

Nick lowered the windows. "Hot," he said.

"Be glad you're not wearing this outfit," Selena said. "It's like being in a sauna."

"Nick, Abidi is coming out of the house."

"Copy."

He started the car, waited for a truck to pass by and made a U-turn back toward the villa. They saw the white BMW ahead and followed it back toward Beirut.

Selena was reading the Arabic documents that Elizabeth had sent.

"The villa belongs to someone called Al-Bayati," Selena said.

"Never heard of him."

"I have," Elizabeth said over the interlink. "He deals in black market information. Classified weapons technology, industrial spying, things like that."

"Sounds like a real philanthropist," Nick said.

"Go talk to Abidi."

"Copy, Director."

CHAPTER 12

The heat of the night was offset by a cooling breeze from the Mediterranean. They'd parked half a block down from Abidi's building. A sodium filled street light reflected from the green storefront on the ground floor, painting the sidewalk a sickly color.

Their dust-streaked Mercedes attracted no attention. The German cars were popular in Lebanon. Three others parked on the block were almost identical.

"A lot of activity in that store," Diego said.

"It's a Hezbollah front. Anybody in there is trouble."

"Going to be hard getting through that."

"We're not going through that," Nick said. "We'll wait for him to come out."

He looked at his watch. "It's early yet. Nothing gets going here till 10 o'clock. Chances are he'll come out for the nightlife like he did the night before last. It's the thing to do here."

"If he doesn't?"

"Then we'll come back tomorrow."

An hour later Yusuf Abidi came out with his bodyguards. Abidi wore dark slacks, polished shoes, sunglasses, a white shirt with a long pointed collar and a linen sport jacket. He had a thick gold chain around his neck. He was joking with one of the guards.

"Man about town," Ronnie said.

The white BMW pulled up and Abidi got in with the guards. Nick waited until the car was a block away before pulling out to follow. The BMW was easy to keep in sight. They headed east, out of the Muslim section of the city. After twenty minutes the car pulled up in front of a nightclub. A line of men and women stretched from the entrance, corralled behind a red velvet rope. A very large man stood at the entrance letting people enter according to some inner criteria. The men were dressed in ways similar to Abidi. The women were about as far away from the Muslim standard of dress as could be. The scene could have been in Paris or New York.

Diego whistled. "Whoa, those women are hot."

They were. High heels, short skirts and low cut blouses seemed to be the norm. Nick thought he saw a pattern about who got in and who was turned away. Hot was in. Not so hot was out.

Abidi got out of his car with his bodyguards. The bouncer held everyone back while the arms dealer went into the club.

"We passed an alley next to the club," Ronnie said. "There has to be a side entrance."

"I see what you're thinking," Nick said. "Get him into the alley and take him somewhere where we can talk to him."

"You got it."

"How do you plan to do that?" Selena asked.

Nick and Ronnie looked at each other. "Use you as bait," Nick said.

"You've got to be kidding."

"You can lose the scarf and do something with the outfit you're wearing under that long dress," Nick said. "This isn't the Muslim section."

"You want me to go in there?"

"I'll go with you."

"I don't think that's a good idea. You don't look like you belong and you don't speak Arabic."

"I can speak it," Diego said. "I can pass for someone who might be from the Middle East."

"Where did you learn Arabic?" Selena asked.

"I picked it up in Afghanistan. I was going to try for Delta. Those guys all have to speak two or three languages."

Nick drove past the club as they talked. Two blocks away he pulled to the curb and let the engine idle.

"Diego, you go in with her. Leave the talking to Selena. Bribe the bouncer. With Selena's looks it should be all right. Ronnie and I will stay with the car and be ready to roll."

"If they let us in, what do you want me to do?" Selena asked.

"Find Abidi and get him outside. This is our best bet. We can't take him at his building."

"We could go after him in his car," Diego said.

"We could. But it will mean a shoot out on the street. You saw what those guards are packing. He's not going to start something in there, it's too crowded."

"Makes sense."

"Selena, what do you think?"

"How do we get into these situations, anyway? I guess there isn't a better choice."

"Think of it as a chance to show off your acting skills."

"The only acting I ever did was as a daffodil in the first grade."

"Then it's time to upgrade your resumé."

CHAPTER 13

Selena changed in the car. The scarf was the first thing to go. She shed the drab dress, revealing a blue silk blouse and short black skirt she was wearing underneath.

She handed Nick her pistol.

"You'd better take this."

"You might need it."

"Where am I supposed to put it? If this works, Abidi will be groping me in no time. A Sig isn't what he wants to feel."

"You have a point," Nick said, "but I don't much like it."

"The groping or leaving the pistol?"

"Both."

"Remember, this was your idea."

She ruffled her hair with her fingers and looked in the car mirror. The way her hair was cut made it easy to turn it into something a little wild.

"You're lucky I like to be prepared," she said. "Hand me my bag."

From the bag she took out a pair of black spike heels and put them on. Usually Selena wore little makeup. This situation called for something different. She looked through a small cosmetics bag and chose a lipstick that accentuated her full lips. She did something with her eyes. All of it only took a few minutes.

When she got out of the car, the transformation was startling. She looked ready for a night in Beirut.

"Whoa," Diego said.

Ronnie whistled.

Nick scratched his ear. "Be careful," he said.

She walked to the head of the line with Diego and smiled at the bouncer. Diego slipped him a hundred dollars American. A minute later they were inside.

The club was a converted industrial warehouse, the interior huge and jammed with people. The roof overhead was thirty feet high, lined with exposed steel rafters and metal scaffolding crowded with banks of stage lights. A hothouse atmosphere of body odor, alcohol and lust assaulted their senses. A polished floor bigger than three or four basketball courts was a swirling sea of sweating people dancing to loud rock music. The volume bordered on painful.

Colored lights swept over the crowd pulsing in time to the music and drenching the dancers in purple, green, yellow and red. From time to time the lights changed to a bright white strobe rhythm that painted the room in frozen flashes of black and white. A raised stage dominated one end of the dance floor where a DJ looked down on the horde of dancers. He grinned like a demonic maestro conducting an orchestra of the damned, rocking to the rhythms and adjusting lights and music as the mood suited him.

To the left of the room was a long bar where people stood shoulder to shoulder three and four deep, holding their drinks and shouting at each other over the noise. To the right was an area crowded with tables. Beyond the tables was a roped off section with couches of red leather. Selena spotted Abidi on one of the couches. He had a drink in his hand. A blonde with large breasts straining against a red blouse sat close to him on his left. His guards stood nearby, watching the crowd.

"I see him," Selena said. "On the couch next to the blonde."

"Looks like he's having a good time." Diego scanned the room. "The alley exit is over there. Right past the couches and next to the restrooms." He paused. "How do you want to play it?"

"He hasn't seen us yet. Why don't you get us drinks. We'll separate. You get over by the restrooms and be ready. Make sure that door will open. I'll convince him that a quickie in the alley with a handsome guy like him would be fun."

Diego raised his eyebrows. "Handsome? He looks like something out of a bad 70s movie set in Miami."

"Men like him are predictable," she said. "I'll have to deal with the competition and it might take a little while to get the message across. Just be ready to move. His bodyguards may decide to come along for the show. That's where you come in. Don't leave me out there in the alley with that creep and his goons by myself."

She touched the transceiver in her ear. "Nick, did you copy that?"

Static. "Copy."

"Why don't you get me a martini?" she said to Diego. "Vodka."

"Shaken or stirred?"

"Do I look like James Bond? Just so long as it's wet."

Diego laughed. A few minutes later he was back with the drinks. Selena took the glass and sipped.

"Lousy vodka." Selena felt the adrenaline rush kick in, the fine high that was like no other she'd ever experienced. It was one of the things that kept her working for Elizabeth.

"Let's do it," she said to Diego.

Outside in the Mercedes, Nick drove around the block until he came back to the front of the club. The line at the door had gotten longer. It stretched toward them and around the corner, away from the side with the alley. He eased past the club and stopped at the alley entrance. The Mercedes was just one more car double parked on the wide street.

"I should be in there with her," Nick said.

"She's got Diego. She's fine."

"You think he can handle it?"

"Yeah. So do you or you wouldn't have sent him in with her."

"When this goes down it's going to be quick."

"It's always quick," Ronnie said.

Inside the club Diego sauntered over to the alley door with his drink. He shielded the door with his body and tried the handle. He felt the latch open and the door move. Gently he pulled it shut. He watched Selena.

Selena talked her way past the first guard and stood in front of Abidi.

"I think I know you," she said in Arabic. "Weren't you at Ibrahim's party?"

It was a gamble. Ibrahim was a common name. If he'd been to a party, it opened the door. If he hadn't, she was ready for that as well.

"I don't remember seeing you there," Abidi said.

Jackpot.

"I remember you," she said. "You were with a different woman."

"What woman?" the blonde said.

"Adara..."

Abidi held up his hand. He looked guilty.

"You son of a bitch. That's the last straw. I've had enough of your lies and women."

She stood and looked at Selena. "Good luck, honey. You're going to need it."

Arabic or English, it's all the same with men like this, Selena thought.

Out in the Mercedes, Nick heard Diego's voice in his ear.

"The woman that was sitting next to Abidi just stomped off, pissed. He's patting the couch. Selena is sitting down. Game on."

"Copy."

"I didn't mean to upset her," Selena said.

She turned toward Abidi, enough to pull her blouse a little lower. He looked at her breasts and then at her face. She smiled.

"You like what you see? Why don't you buy me another drink?"

"Forgive me, what are you drinking?"

"Vodka martini."

Abidi signaled one of his guards.

"A vodka martini for my companion. Make sure they give her the good vodka, not that crap they usually serve."

"The good vodka?"

"You heard me."

The man nodded and moved off toward the bar.

"You are quite lovely," Abidi said. "I don't understand why I don't remember you."

"I think you may have had a bit to drink. I know I did. It was quite a party."

"It was. I'm Yusuf."

"Fatima."

"Ah, one of the four perfect women."

"Only in name," Selena said.

"You enjoy parties, Fatima? I am going to one later. Perhaps you would like to accompany me?"

The guard came back with Selena's drink. She took it and sipped. It was a vast improvement over the first one.

"I think I'd like that," she said.

She reached over and touched the gold chain around his neck. She played with the hairs on his chest.

"Do we have to wait until later to party?"

She sipped her martini. It really was very good and the drink helped with her nervousness. She took another sip.

This is going to be easy, she thought.

Yusuf gave her a calculating look. "What did you have in mind?"

She whispered in his ear. Yusuf smiled.

"I'm going to use the ladies room," she said.

"I will be waiting for you."

Yusuf half rose from the couch as Selena got up and walked away.

The guard who had brought Selena's drink said, "I do not trust her."

"No, Gibril, nor do I. She is either a whore or a spy. Either way, I am going to enjoy her. Go get the car and take it around back. Hassan will stay here with me. You put the drug in her drink?"

"Of course."

"Good. Go."

Diego had moved a few yards from the door to the alley and away from the restrooms. He watched Selena get up and walk unsteadily to the toilets. He triggered his comm link.

"Nick, I think Selena is drunk."

"That can't be," Nick answered. "You haven't been there long enough. Besides, she wouldn't compromise an operation."

"She just went into the bathroom and she's walking like she is. Abidi sent one of his guards away. Now he's getting up and coming toward the alley door with the other one."

"Maybe she's pretending, to get him off guard," Nick said.

"I don't think so. You can't fake the way she looks."

Nick's ear began itching. Ronnie saw him reach up to scratch it.

"I'll bet the son of a bitch drugged her," Nick said. "I'm going into the alley. Don't let that other guard follow her."

"Copy that," Diego said.

"You want me to go with you?" Ronnie asked.

"No. Stay with the car and keep it running. We may have to leave in a hurry."

Nick got out of the car, left the door ajar and entered the narrow alley. It was dark away from the street. The alley was paved with cobbled stones and went all the way through to the next street over. A rusted bell shaped fixture set over the alley door cast a week pool of yellow light into the darkness.

A white car stopped at the far end of the alley. Nick recognized Abidi's BMW.

Shit.

He spoke into the comm link.

"Ronnie, Diego, Selena's been made. It's a set up. Abidi's car is at the other end of the alley. The driver and the guard are getting out. They're coming into the alley."

Nick pressed against the rough stone wall in the shadows of the alley, hoping he hadn't been seen.

He took out his SIG .40, pulled back the hammer and laid his finger alongside the receiver.

It was about ten yards to the alley door. The door opened and Selena staggered out, her arm gripped tightly by Abidi and followed by one of the guards. The two men at the other end of the alley began walking faster. Then Diego came through the open door. He piled into the guard. The door slammed shut behind them. Diego and the guard went down onto the stones and dirt.

Abidi shouted. Guns came out at the other end of the alley and Nick fired. He missed, fired again and one of the two went down. The shots echoed in the narrow confines of the buildings. The second man opened fire. Nick felt the rounds pass by. He crouched down and let off three quick shots that took Abidi's man in the chest and knocked him aside. The first man was getting to his feet. Nick shot him again, twice. He stopped trying to get up.

Abidi held Selena in front of him as a shield. He held an ugly curved knife an inch from her throat, gleaming under the light over the door. Her head lolled to the side. Her eyes were open, unfocused. Nick stood.

"Stop," Abidi said. "I will kill her."

Nick still held the gun in his right hand. Diego got to his feet and froze in place, standing over the unconscious body of the bodyguard. Out on the street someone was shouting. In minutes, police would be swarming the scene.

"Okay," Nick said.

Then he shot Abidi in the head.

The .40 caliber hollow point blew out the back of Yusuf's skull. His arms flew wide and he went backward. Diego caught Selena as she crumpled to the ground. Nick ran forward.

"Get her to the car," he said.

They each took an arm and half carried, half dragged her back to the idling Mercedes. One of her black shoes came off in the alley. Ronnie had the doors open for them. He climbed back into the driver's seat as they threw Selena into the back. Nick got in with her. Diego jumped into the front.

As soon as they were inside the car, Ronnie peeled away from the curb. Somewhere in the distance sirens sounded.

"How is she?" Ronnie said.

"Out of it. They used something strong. She's going to be sick when she wakes up."

"That was a hell of a shot, Nick," Diego said.

"He had the knife away from her throat. I wouldn't have taken it if the blade was right up against her."

"Just the same, a hell of a shot."

After twenty minutes they were back in front of their hotel.

"Time to check out," Nick said. "You two clear out the rooms. I'll give the pilot a heads-up and stay in the car with her."

Later, on the way to the airport, Selena threw up.

Nick left the car in the parking lot outside the private terminal where their plane waited. They boarded the Gulf Stream without incident. Twenty minutes later they were in the air. Selena fell asleep.

Three hours later she was awake, drinking coffee. She held a cloth wrapped around ice on her head.

"What happened?" she said.

"You were drugged. What do you remember?"

"Abidi's man brought me a drink. I remember thinking it tasted a lot better than the one I'd ordered at the bar. I just sipped it. Then I remember whispering in Yusuf's ear, trying to get him into the alley. He was wearing this awful cologne."

"Then what?"

"I had to go to the bathroom. The next thing I knew I was throwing up in the car."

"Yeah, that was a mess. When the rental people find that Mercedes they're not going to be happy. We left it in the parking lot."

"What happened to Abidi?"

"He's dead."

Nick told her about the fight in the alley.

"I thought I had him fooled," Selena said. "I guess I'm not so smart after all."

"Don't blame yourself. It was always a long shot."

She looked out the window. There was nothing to see except the night sky. Out here over the Atlantic, away from civilization, the stars were bright. Banks of clouds passed below the plane.

"He could have raped me. I could have been killed."

"He didn't and you weren't. That's what counts. We were there to back you up."

"This time. What happens if you're not?"

"You can't think about it like that. I've seen what you can do. You can handle yourself if things get dicey."

"That's what I've always thought," Selena said. "After they gave me that drug I was helpless. What good is all my training if I can't even stand up?"

"I don't have a good answer for that."

"I wish you did."

Selena closed her eyes and lay back in her seat. Nick watched her.

What if I hadn't been there? he thought.

He imagined what could have happened to her and forced the images out of his mind.

CHAPTER 14

"Did you have to kill him, Nick? You were just supposed to question him."

"I didn't have a choice."

Elizabeth sighed. It was two days later. No one had made the connection between the foreigners visiting Beirut and Yusuf Abidi's death. It was just one more murder in a city that had seen thousands die over the past decades. Life was cheap in Beirut.

"All right. Moving on, Stephanie thinks she's found something," Elizabeth said.

"We know that the man who wrote the scroll was named Ephram," Stephanie said. "I plugged that into the computers and set search parameters for the first century CE. There was an Ephram back then who was part of the revolt against Rome. I think he's the one who made that scroll. He wrote in Aramaic, which fits. The Romans caught him the year after they took Jerusalem."

"Sounds like our guy," Nick said. "What happened to him?"

"He was crucified."

"Did you find anything that might lead us to the tomb?" Selena asked.

"There's another scroll in the British Museum written by Ephram that mentions the Queen of Sheba. There are stories that connect Sheba and Solomon, so there might be something in that. It's the only thing I found that might be related."

"I thought Sheba was a legend," Diego said.

"Most scholars think she was real," Selena said, "although they argue about it, like everything else in the Old Testament. She probably ruled in what's now Yemen. Some think it was Egypt or Ethiopia. In the Bible she visits Solomon, bringing treasure as gifts. She's called the black queen in some legends and the Queen of the South in the Gospels. That could be anywhere south of Galilee. A lot of different cultures claim her for their own."

"I couldn't find out much about the scroll in the British Museum," Stephanie said. "There's no translation posted, just a note that it mentions Sheba. It was written by Ephram around the same time as the other one. I know it's a reach. It's all I could find."

"It might be worth checking out," Elizabeth said.

"We should go look at it," Selena said. "With my academic credentials they'll let me see it. I'll tell them it's research for a lecture."

Elizabeth nodded. "Go ahead and set it up."

"What's the next move, Director," Nick asked.

"You followed Abidi to the compound of a man named Al-Bayati," Elizabeth said. "The connection with Abidi makes him our only lead at the moment. I decided to take a closer look at him. Steph, run the shots."

The first picture on the monitor was of Al-Bayati.

"Meet one of the thorns in Langley's side," Elizabeth said.

The picture was in black and white, taken from a distance. It was clear enough to show the brutality in Al-Bayati's features. His head was large, with jutting brows and a sloped forehead. His hair was black and thick. His arms seemed unusually long and powerful, almost simian.

"Primitive looking dude," Diego said. "Reminds me of a guy I knew a long time ago, back in Colorado."

"You're from Colorado?" Ronnie asked.

"Born and raised. I come from outside of Fort Collins, north of Denver. My grandfather emigrated there from Mexico back in the 40s. He grew beets. Now the water's been ripped off and the land's dried up. It would break his heart if he could see it."

Elizabeth tapped her pen.

"Let's stay focused. Al-Bayati sells classified information to the wrong people. Hezbolla protects him and leaves him alone because Tehran tells them to. As you heard from Lucas, he sells black-market arms and stolen technology. There are disturbing rumors about him but no one has ever been able to substantiate them."

"What kind of rumors?" Ronnie asked.

"That children go into his villa in Lebanon and never come out again."

"Sounds like a charming fellow," Selena said

"He seldom leaves his villa. Show us the house, Steph."

The picture changed to show Bayati's sprawling mansion, set on a steep cliff overlooking the Mediterranean. The villa had the classic look of whitewashed walls and red tiled roof. It had been built in the shape of a U around a tiled courtyard. The open part of the U featured a broad fountain surrounded by shade trees and manicured shrubbery. On the Mediterranean side, a wide patio behind the main part of the house ended at a large pool. Beyond the pool a triple row of gleaming razor wire lined the edge of the cliff. Hundreds of feet below, the dark waves of the Mediterranean

Sea crashed and foamed against jagged rocks rising up from the water.

The cliff and the water formed a security barrier for one side of the compound. The other three sides were protected by a high, whitewashed stone wall topped with loops of razor wire and shards of broken glass. There was one entrance in, through a massive iron gate. A guardhouse inside the compound sat next to the gate. Several cars were parked on the left side of the compound.

Nick said, "He has a Quad .50 sitting there in the shade. See it? By the wing where all the cars are?"

"I'll be damned," Ronnie said. "I thought those were all in museums."

The Quad .50 consisted of four Browning .50 caliber machine guns controlled by a motorized turret mounted on a truck or platform. Once those guns opened up, anything in front of them was chopped into mincemeat. Low-flying planes, vehicles, buildings and people stood no chance against it.

"Think it's operational?"

"Bet on it," Nick said. "If we end up going in there we'd better make sure nobody gets a chance to use it."

"That wall must be sixteen feet high if it's an inch," Ronnie said. "That razor wire looks tough."

"The cliff might be the best way in," Diego said. "Looks like about an hour climb, maybe more, depending on the rock. He's got wire there, too, on the edge of the pool."

"You've done a lot of climbing?" Nick asked.

"Free and roped," Diego said. "I like the challenge."

Selena listened to the interchange and thought Diego was fitting right in. He'd proved himself in Beirut. Still it was odd without Lamont here. She wondered if Ramirez had any dive training. With Lamont gone, she was the only one on the team with any serious experience. No one else was qualified for the deep work.

Elizabeth interrupted her thoughts.

"This is early days and we need more intel. Just the same, I want to begin thinking about what it would take to get into that compound and interview Bayati."

"You make it sound like something for the evening news," Ronnie said.

"You know exactly what I mean," Elizabeth said. "Nick, I want you and Selena to leave for London tonight and check out that scroll in the British Museum. You'll fly commercial on your own passports."

"What about weapons? Every time we check our weapons and get to England there's a hassle about claiming them."

"Leave them. You're just going to the museum. I'll arrange something with the embassy just in case. If you start shooting people over there the Brits won't be the only ones who are unhappy. I'll be unhappy. I don't think you want that."

"Diego and Ronnie?" Nick said.

"I want Ronnie here working with Sergeant Ramirez. Ronnie, bring him up to speed on how we do everything around here. There are lots of things he needs to know. Diego, you and Ronnie start working out how you would take that villa if it becomes necessary. When Nick and Selena get back, we'll go over it."

"Copy that, Director."

"Any questions?"
There weren't any.
"Have a good flight, Nick."

CHAPTER 15

Nazar Al-Bayati sat on the patio of his fortified compound and looked out over the Mediterranean at the blazing ball of the sun dropping toward the horizon. He never got tired of the Mediterranean sunsets, especially when the fiery colors were partly obscured by black clouds, as if the world burned. It reminded him of pleasant times spent in the presence of heat and darkness, fire and the sweet smoke of incense.

The scroll was never far from his mind. Solomon had been one of the great ancient magicians, in the tradition of Bayati's ancestors. It was said that objects of power had been buried with him. There was one in particular Bayati sought. If it was in the tomb and if he could find it, the world would be his. Bayati believed in magic. He had seen too many strange phenomena in his life to think that magic wasn't real. Of course it required great skill and preparation to hold and use it. He knew what was required.

Rituals and sacrifices, rites that were older than the pyramids.

Today began a new lunar cycle. Nazar absentmindedly fingered his crotch in anticipation of the ceremony that would take place later. Before then there was business to attend to.

He rose, went into the house and beckoned a servant.

"Find Rhoades and send him to my study."

"At once, Abu."

The man scurried away. Al-Bayati went to a sideboard of rosewood inlaid with gold that stood by the near wall, a piece that had once graced the Emperor Napoleon's private study. He pressed a carved rosette on the corner and a panel slid down on the end, revealing a hidden compartment. A dozen foil wrapped balls the size of marbles rested on a tray inside. Beside them were six glass vials containing tablets of an odd brown color. The last item inside the cabinet was an ancient green bottle.

Al-Bayati took one of the balls and placed it on top of the sideboard on a silver tray. He opened a vial, shook two pills onto his hand and set the vial down. He took two more pills and set them down next to the ball. He took the cork out of the green bottle and washed down the pills with a swallow of the liquid it contained. The liquor burned on its way down. Al-Bayati put the cork back in the bottle, the bottle and the vial back into the cabinet, and touched the rosette again. The panel sprang upward and locked with a sharp click. Al-Bayati sat down in a broad leather chair.

Addison Rhoades came into the room. Al-Bayati felt the first rush of the drugs ripple through him in a wave. The main effect was still an hour away. By then everything would be ready.

"You sent for me?"

"You know about Yusuf?"

Rhoades nodded.

"What happened?"

Rhoades shrugged. "Perhaps he made a deal with the wrong people or gave them the wrong goods."

"I want you to find out who killed him."

"It shouldn't be too hard," Rhoades said. "He was approached by a woman in the club. There are cameras. Nothing in the alley where he died. Plenty of tape from inside."

"Get the tapes. I don't think it was an unhappy client."

"Who else would it be?"

"Who knows? The Israelis, perhaps? However I think they would be more subtle. It may have been someone with an interest in my affairs."

"It's possible," Rhoades said. "I'll look into it."

"Something else. There is another scroll," Al-Bayati said. "I want you to obtain it. It may help us find the tomb."

"Another? Where is it?"

"In the British Museum. Locate it and bring it to me."

Rhoades looked nervous. "It's too late to go today..."

Al-Bayati laughed. "Don't worry, you don't have to go until tomorrow. You know I need you to assist me. Is everything prepared?"

"Yes. The new moon will rise in about forty minutes."

"The boy?"

"In his room. He has already received the drug."

"Good. Go over to the sideboard. You'll find what you need there."

Rhoades walked over to the sideboard and picked up the foil wrapped ball. He popped the pills into his mouth and swallowed them dry.

"Get the boy ready and bring him to my bedroom."

Rhoades left the room and Al-Bayati leaned back in the comfortable chair and closed his eyes, feeling the power of the ancient drugs begin to lift him into a different realm.

The formulas Al-Bayati used to create his heightened awareness dated back thousands of years, to a time when Carthage had been as great as her rival Rome. Nazar believed he was descended from a high priest of Carthage. It was as his father had taught him, as his father had been taught as well, going back in an unbroken line through the millennia.

Carthage had long since turned to dust but the true religion had been kept alive in secret throughout the centuries. There had always been worshipers and priests to serve the god. Now, most of the followers were gone. Nazar was the last of his line, the last who knew the true mysteries. He'd been unable to sire a male heir. If there was one thing in his life he regretted, it was that. Not long ago he had come to the realization that time was running out for him. The women he had coupled with in the past had failed to produce a male child, always it was a girl. The women disappeared. He'd found another use for the girls who were born.

No one had ever bothered to ask what happened to the women. They wouldn't have dared. People didn't ask Nazar Al-Bayati about things like that. He had his eye on a new candidate. If she didn't produce, Al-Bayati had come to the conclusion he would have to choose a successor not of his blood. It was a difficult realization, one he did not want to accept. Tonight's sacrifice would be special, meant to draw the god's favor to him. Surely, his prayer would be answered.

He stood and swayed for a moment as his body adjusted to the drugs. Everything in the room glowed with light and color. The soft touch of his silk robe was like a caress. He could feel the blood coursing through his veins and heat in his groin. The god was not jealous. The boy's virginity was not a requirement.

The power of his youthful blood was what counted.

CHAPTER 16

Selena's reputation as a renowned lecturer in ancient Middle Eastern and Oriental languages opened doors at the British Museum kept closed to the public. The Museum housed one of the greatest collections in existence of Middle Eastern artifacts. There had been a time when British expeditions bent on exploration and discovery had covered the globe. Crumbling ruins no one cared about turned out to be treasure houses of statuary, carvings and cultural artifacts from lost civilizations.

The world had changed since the days of empire. Many of the acquisitions had become controversial. As far as Selena knew, the scroll they were interested in wasn't one of them.

Nick and Selena were met by a man in his fifties wearing a conservative worsted suit. He wore glasses with designer frames that had probably cost close to a thousand dollars. He had a thin, aristocratic face with an expression as though there had been too much lemon in his tea and sported a thin, sandy mustache that reminded Nick of pictures he'd seen of British officers during World War I. He introduced himself as Sir Peter Wainwright. Wainwright was the man in charge of the Department of the Middle East.

"I must say, it's a genuine pleasure to meet you, Doctor Connor. I haven't seen much in the journals from you lately. Your treatise a few years ago on classical Greek was quite intriguing."

"Thank you, Sir Peter. I've been looking forward to meeting you. This is my personal secretary, Nicholas Carter."

Nick and Selena had agreed before going in that he would play the role of gofer and assistant. She'd laughed at his look and promised not to send him out for coffee.

"How do you do?" Wainwright shook hands with Nick.

"Pleasure," Nick said.

Wainwright's handshake was limp and slightly damp. Wainwright turned back to Selena, dismissing him. Nick resisted the urge to dry his hand on his pants.

"I understand you're interested in our scroll by Ephram."

"That's correct."

"May I ask why that scroll in particular? We have many fine examples of Aramaic scrolls."

"I was curious about the reference to the Queen of Sheba," Selena said. "The Museum catalog mentions its presence. There's no further information except to date it to the first century CE."

Wainwright pursed his lips. "Space in the catalog is at something of a premium. It was felt that it merited only a listing."

"And the content?" Selena probed.

"It's a rather uninspired travel diary. Perhaps it's better if you look at it yourself. I confess that I have never read it."

"Then how do you know what's in it?" Nick said.

Selena gave him a warning look.

Wainwright sniffed.

"There are good people under me upon whom I rely," he said. "My specialty is cuneiform."

"Of course," Nick said. "A foolish question."

Selena looked at him again. He smiled at her.

"This way," Wainwright said.

He led them past two winged lions with human heads flanking a short hall. The hall ended at a magnificent wooden gate placed against the wall.

"Those are from Nimrud in Iraq," Wainwright said. "About 860 BCE or thereabouts."

"Impressive," Nick said. "Those lions would look pretty good at the entrance to somebody's driveway."

Selena rolled her eyes. Wainwright ignored him. They came to an unmarked door. Wainwright took out a set of keys and opened it. He led them through a room filled with shelves stacked with boxed and numbered artifacts. There was a wooden work table. Wainwright reached up to a shelf above it.

"Here we are," Wainwright said. "You're in luck. The Ephram scroll was recently prepared for display as an example of the daily tedium of a trading caravan from the period and writing typical of the era. And of course there's the brief mention of the Queen of Sheba. That adds interest. There's damage, however I'm told it's quite readable."

The ancient parchment had been unrolled and mounted flat in a glass box filled with inert gas. It was about four feet long and a little over a foot high. Rips and holes broke up the narrative in several places. The last part of the scroll was little more than fragments. Narrow lines of tiny writing covered the visible surface.

"Where was it discovered?" Selena asked.

"In Egypt, during the nineteenth century," Wainwright said. "It was found with several other scrolls in a villa dating from the time of Cleopatra."

"When the Romans were there."

"Yes."

"Do the Egyptians want it back?"

"They do. They've been waiting for it, along with everything else we have here that came from Egypt. I'm afraid they'll have rather a long wait."

"This is a very odd construction," Selena said. She pointed at a section of writing where something seemed to have eaten part of the parchment. "I've never seen anything quite like it before."

"I don't read Aramaic," Wainwright said. "I'll take your word for it."

"I'd like to photograph this if it's all right with you. It's going to take some time for me to make an accurate translation. I'll be sure to send you my results and comments if you'd like."

"Of course, Doctor Connor." Wainwright looked at his watch. "Tea time. Would the two of you care for a cup of tea?"

"That would be wonderful. Thank you, Sir Peter."

"How do you take it?"

"Milk on the bottom, please."

Wainwright nodded approvingly. "And you, Mister Carter?"

"I'll take a coffee if you have one," Nick said. "Black."

Wainwright sniffed again. "I'll see what I can do. Let me go find someone to get it for us."

He left them at the table and disappeared between the shelves.

"Are you deliberately trying to piss him off?" Selena asked when Wainwright was out of earshot. "First that crack about the lions and now you want coffee?"

"He's annoying," Nick said. "I don't like the way he looks at you. Besides, I don't like tea that much."

"You're hopeless."

Selena took out her phone and began photographing the scroll.

"What does it say?" Nick asked.

"Like I told Sir Peter, it will take me a little time to translate it. From what I can see, it's just what he said, a diary of a trading expedition south into the Arabian Peninsula from Jerusalem."

"Carrying the body of Solomon?"

"There's no mention that I can see," Selena said. She pointed. "This is the reference to the Queen of Sheba. It's in the section that's torn and there's something strange about the way it's written. I'll have to study it to make any sense of what it means."

Wainwright returned. "Have you managed to complete your pictures, Doctor Connor? I've asked that tea be laid out for us in the canteen."

"I'm almost done." She took two more pictures and put her phone back in her purse. "I could use a nice cup of tea."

An hour later they were coming down the steps of the museum. Neither Nick nor Selena noticed the tall man who glanced at them as he passed them going up.

CHAPTER 17

The next morning Nick and Selena went out for breakfast. Their plane wasn't leaving until the afternoon. They passed a newsstand.

"Nick. Look at that headline."

MURDER AT THE BRITISH MUSEUM

Nick bought a paper and glanced at the article. "Guess who was murdered?"

"Not Sir Peter?"

"Right the first time. Somebody cut his throat. I didn't like him much but he didn't deserve that."

"It can't be a coincidence," Selena said.

"No."

"Does it say anything about the scroll?"

Nick scanned the article. "It says an inventory is being conducted and police suspect theft as the motive."

"Somebody killed him and took the scroll," Selena said.

"It looks that way. Good thing you have those pictures."

"It has to be the same people who blew up the train and the research facility in Grenoble."

"Seems likely." Nick looked at his watch. "A little early in Virginia to call Harker."

"You think she'll want us to stay here?"

"I don't see any reason why she would. Wainwright's dead and I'll bet the scroll is gone. There's nothing we can do about it on this end."

"What about breakfast?"

"That's one of the things I like about you," he said. "The way you pay attention to what's important. We'll eat, go back to the hotel and get to the airport. I'll call Harker from there."

Five hours later they were over the Atlantic headed home. The business class seats on the British Airways 777 were wide and comfortable. Selena sipped a Mimosa and began making notes as she worked through the pictures she'd taken of the scroll, reading the story.

Ephram had left Jerusalem with a trading caravan in the same year the Romans reached the city, headed to the southern part of the Arabian Peninsula and what was now Yemen. There was no mention of Solomon or anything to do with the Temple. She came to the part of the scroll that seemed odd to her. Selena was familiar with many variations of classical and biblical Aramaic. She'd never seen anything like what Ephram had written.

"This is really interesting," she said.

Nick sat next to her. He was nursing a glass of whiskey and reading about the gadgets offered in one of the magazines provided by the airline.

"What is?"

"This part of the scroll." She tapped her finger on the notes she had made. "It just doesn't make sense. Up until this point it's typical Aramaic, then suddenly it becomes unreadable. It's almost as if the letters were scrambled."

"Maybe they are," Nick said.

"Why would Ephram..." Selena paused. "Oh. You think it's deliberate. A code?"

"It could be. Maybe he's hiding something."

"Like where he hid the treasure?"

"At least something he didn't want people to know about. Why did he go on that trip in the first place?" Nick asked.

"Rome was advancing on the city. This caravan could be the one that took Solomon's body out of Jerusalem. The scroll says it was carrying cloth and wine to the south. I have trouble believing that. Why go overland? If you were a trader back then, it was easier and quicker to sail down to the southern tip of Arabia with your cargo. Ephram's route went down the eastern side of the coastal range in Arabia, through the kingdom of the Dedanites. They're the ones mentioned in the other scroll. It's hard to believe he'd take that route to sell goods."

"Maybe he had a stake in the profits. They must have needed money to fight the Romans."

"I don't see how a trip to the bottom of Arabia would help. It's a long way from Jerusalem and Judea, especially in those days."

"No mention of Solomon?"

"None. Only the reference to the Queen of Sheba. The section I can't read comes right after that."

"What does Ephram say about Sheba?"

"That she was the Queen of the Night. Then he says that those who follow the route to her home will find wisdom."

"That's all he says?"

Selena nodded. She finished her Mimosa and signaled the attendant for another.

"The mention of Sheba seems out of context," she said. "It doesn't make any sense. That's right where everything becomes garbled in the narrative. Part of that section is damaged and can't be read at all. Then the narrative picks up again and Ephram starts talking about the coast of Arabia. He calls it a terrible country and says that hostile tribes live in the mountains. There's nothing else of interest to us that I can see. The end of the narrative is illegible. It looks like something ate part of the scroll."

The attendant brought Selena's drink.

"If that section is in code it can't be that complicated," Nick said. "Those old codes worked great back then but they're child's play compared to the modern stuff. Give it to Stephanie when we get back and have her run it through the computers. If it's a code, she should be able to crack it."

Selena gathered up her notes and put them away.

"How come you're not using your laptop?" Nick said.

"I like the feel of pen and paper. It's more personal and I think better that way. Once I know what I want to say, that's when I go to the computer."

"Kind of old-fashioned," Nick said.

"That's me. How long do you plan to keep Diego on probation?" she asked.

"You think he fits?"

"He's not afraid to say what he thinks and he does have the skills we need."

"He did a good job in Beirut. I'm giving him a qualified yes. He has a quick temper. That could cause trouble if he doesn't control it."

"So he's still on probation."

"For the time being. Besides, it will keep him on his toes."

"I wonder how Lamont is doing?"

"He's leasing a dive shop in Florida," Nick said. "I talked to him a couple of days ago. He sounded bored."

"Compared to what we do, just about anything is boring."

"Yeah, like that old Chinese curse about living in interesting times. Interesting times meant the barbarians were about to ride over your fields and kill you and your family. In old China nobody wanted things to be interesting."

"Would you rather be bored?"

"No," Nick said. Just the same I wouldn't mind if things were a little less interesting, at least in that department."

He paused. "I've been thinking."

"That's a change."

"No, really. I've been thinking about us getting married."

There was something in the tone of his voice that was different. Selena felt a jolt in her stomach. What was he going to say?

"I think we should do it soon."

"You do?"

"I was thinking maybe September or October. While the weather's still good."

"Why? I mean, why now?"

"You don't want to get married?"

"No. I mean, yes, I want to get married. What changed your mind? You've been putting it off."

Nick looked out the window and turned back to her. "So have you."

It was true. He wasn't the only one who'd been ambivalent about taking the final step.

Nick continued. "I've been putting it off because I still had some feelings I had to work through."

"What feelings?"

"You know I worry about one of us getting killed. We talked about that. After Megan, I shut everything down. I didn't want to feel like that again."

Selena nodded. Megan had been the love of Nick's life. He'd watched her die in a meaningless plane crash.

"I remember when my parents and my brother died," Selena said. "I didn't think I'd ever be happy again or that I could ever let myself feel love again because it was just too painful. I guess what I'm saying is I've been holding back for pretty much the same reasons you have."

"Hell, nobody gets out of here alive. Sooner or later something is going to get us. Life's too short. I love you. Getting married seems like a good way to prove it."

"You don't have to prove anything." She leaned over and kissed him. "I know where there's a nice church in Alexandria."

"You already picked out a church?"

"Just in case. If you don't like it we'll find somewhere else."

The flight attendant stopped by their seats. "Can I get you another Mimosa?" he asked.

They both spoke at the same time. "Yes." "Sure."

When the drinks came Nick held his glass up. "To us."

"To us."

CHAPTER 18

Lucas Monroe couldn't quite get used to his new office on the seventh floor. It was large and spacious, soundproofed and paneled in polished wood, almost the same size as the Director's. Lucas liked the quiet but he missed the socializing that took place on the lower floors. Now he was isolated behind secretaries and protocols. It went with the territory. It didn't mean he had to like it. Being important wasn't all it was cracked up to be.

All of a sudden his life was filled with changes. This promotion. The baby. Especially the baby. He was looking forward to the birth with mixed dread and anticipation. The only thing he was certain of was that the baby meant change. Stephanie was happy and that went a long way to balance his anxiety.

In some ways it had been easier when he was a field agent in Afghanistan and everyone was trying to kill him.

His intercom buzzed.

"Yes, Angela."

"The DCI is on line two."

"Thank you."

He touched the blinking button on his phone.

"Director."

"I've just received an inquiry from Jerusalem," Hood said. "The Israelis want to find out what we know about the scroll that was x-rayed in France."

"That didn't take long," Lucas said.

"What do you think we should tell them?"

"If we tell them anything it should come through Harker," Lucas said. "She's the point on this. If there's anything involving the Israelis, she's the one to do it."

"You're still convinced that's the best course of action?"

"I am. Nothing has changed. This situation has the potential to turn into a political and media nightmare. We don't want to be in the middle of that if it happens. Harker has the protection of the president and she's been in hot spots before. You know what she's done, better than most."

"I just wanted to make sure you still felt the same way."

"Where did the request come from?"

"Mossad."

"If they're asking about the scroll, they know what's on it and are fishing to see if we know more. If I were the Israelis, I'd be thinking about mounting an operation to go after that tomb."

"They have to find it first," Hood said.

"Once they figure out where it's supposed to be, I don't think there's any way to stop them. The best we can hope for is to know what they're going to do and when they're going to do it. That way we can intervene if we need to."

"And how do you propose to find that out?"

"I think we should let Harker tell them what we know, which isn't much. All we really know is that the scroll says the Temple relics and Solomon's remains were taken south into what's now Saudi Arabia. It doesn't say anything more than that. There's nothing specific. Mossad will have translated the scroll so we won't be telling them anything new. If we cooperate with them now they might work with us later if it gets complicated."

"That's not necessarily true. The Israelis can be very stubborn."

"We have nothing to lose at this point. They're still our allies."

"Only when our interests coincide," Hood said.

"You can't expect them to be any different. Our two countries don't always want the same thing. At least we're agreed on one fundamental."

"What's that?"

"Anything that leads to a major war in the Middle East is bad news. I think we should pass the connection on to Harker and let her know she can tell them whatever she thinks is right."

"I don't think she would do anything else," Hood said. "If I've learned one thing about Elizabeth it's that you're not going to tell her how to think or what to do."

Lucas laughed. "That makes her a perfect match for the Israelis."

CHAPTER 19

Addison Rhoades woke feeling as if someone had hit him in the head with an axe. His mouth tasted like camel dung and sand. His tongue was swollen. He could smell his breath, foul and unpleasant. He stumbled out of bed and into the bathroom. He used the toilet and turned on the shower. One of the advantages to living in Al-Bayati's villa was hot water, even if the pressure left something to be desired.

His career at MI6 had ended under a cloud. He'd been in Iraq. Two prisoners had died while he was interrogating them. Whitehall had adopted Washington's new policy of politically correct treatment of enemies. Rhoades had an IQ approaching genius level. It didn't take a high IQ to see that after the incident in Iraq his days in the service were numbered.

American dollars had poured into Iraq by the planeload after Hussein was defeated. Washington threw money at the corporations, security firms and corrupt Iraqis who were supposed to turn the country into an American extension of the oil industry. Accurate accounting was almost nonexistent. Rhoades had arranged for several million dollars to be diverted to an account in the Cayman Islands, in anticipation of the day he'd be terminated.

It had been a smart move. Rhoades had hidden embarrassing proof about what was going on in Iraq and threatened to release it publicly. A deal had been struck. The hypocrites who ran MI6 waived prosecution and any attempts to recover the money.

In return he'd resigned and promised not to release his information.

For the good of the service, they'd said.

As he walked out the door of MI6 headquarters for the last time, he made a decision. If he couldn't work for them, he would work against them. His years in the Middle East had left him with a wide base of contacts. Within a year he was well-established as a man who could be relied on to persuade someone of what was in their best interests and remove them as a problem if they could not be convinced. Then he and Al-Bayati had found each other. That had been three years before.

Now warning bells were sounding in his mind. Rhoades had a well-developed ability to see trouble coming before others knew it. It had gotten him out of situations that would have ended badly for most men.

He stood under the shower for a long time, his mind clearing under the flowing water. The night before had been unusually disturbing. Al-Bayati's behavior was becoming more erratic, more extreme. Standing under the water, Rhoades faced the thought that had been nagging him for months.

He's insane. He really is.

Addison Rhoades was under no illusions about his own perverted morality, but Al-Bayati had gone beyond what even he could tolerate. Nazar's brutal and sexually sadistic nature was sliding out of control. That was bad enough. What had convinced him was when Al-Bayati had told him the real reason he wanted to find the tomb and Solomon.

It wasn't just the money, the enormous treasure that was supposed to be buried with the king. It wasn't even the potential profit in exploiting an explosive political situation where all the major players in the Middle East had a stake in the outcome. It was because of something rumored to have been buried with Solomon.

A ring. More specifically, a magic ring, bearing the Seal of Solomon.

In Jewish, Islamic and Western occultism, Solomon's ring had magical powers for good and evil. Legend held that Solomon could bring the desert wind with the ring. He could call upon the jinni, the dark spirits of the desert. He could speak with animals.

Al-Bayati wanted the power he thought that ring would bring him.

Working for a madman who sought to retrieve a magical ring was not Rhoades' cup of tea. It was time to think about finding new employment. He'd miss the drugs but he'd been there before. A week or two of unpleasantness and he would be past it. Besides, there were other drugs to ease the transition. In the meantime, he needed to make sure Al-Bayati had no reason to suspect his loyalty. If Nazar became suspicious, the results would be most unpleasant.

Rhoades turned off the water, stepped out of the shower stall and began to dry off. He thought about the scroll. Even though he was certain that Solomon's ring was a myth, the treasure of the Jewish Temple was not.

The ancient Hebrews, like many other peoples of the time, believed that God was pleased and honored by the gleam of gold. The Temple had been filled with treasures made from the precious metal, a horde unlike anything else in history.

Religion had changed since the destruction of the Temple. One thing that had stayed the same was the worship of gold. It was as strong as ever.

Rhoades didn't believe in magic or religion but he believed in gold. As long as Al-Bayati was looking for the hidden tomb, he would bide his time. Why not let him do the work, using his network of spies? If anyone could find it, it would be Nazar, Rhoades was certain. When the tomb was discovered he'd make his move.

He finished drying his hair and looked at himself in the mirror. Even with the dark bags under his eyes he thought he was still an attractive man, though some would say the mirror revealed his dissolution. There seemed to be more lines today than usual. His eyes were bloodshot, that was to be expected. It was a small price to pay for pleasure.

The gold in that tomb would buy anything he wanted for the rest of his life. Women, boys, a villa in the islands, youth. Anything he wanted.

He smiled at his reflection.

Rhoades dressed and went down the main staircase to the grand entrance of Al-Bayati's villa. He put on sunglasses and walked back to the patio where Al-Bayati lay by the pool.

It was midmorning. The full strength of the sun had not made itself felt. Even so Rhoades felt sweat break out on his forehead. Al-Bayati lay on his lounge chair covered with glistening oil, like a beached, hairy creature from some dark sea.

"What is it?" he said.

"I found out who came after Yusuf."

"Go on."

"I don't know who was in the alley. Witnesses said there were three men involved. One of them was in the club, along with the woman."

"Get to the point."

Rhoades resisted a sudden urge to reach into his pocket for the switchblade he always carried and cut the disrespectful bastard's throat from ear to ear. He filed the thought away for another time.

"They were Americans."

Al-Bayati sat up. "Americans? Who? CIA?"

"No, another group, much smaller. Another intelligence unit, not well publicized. I identified the woman from a picture taken inside the club."

Al-Bayati was many things but he was far from stupid. "They're after information about the scrolls," he said.

"It would appear so. When I looked at the video from the club, I knew I'd seen her somewhere. She was leaving the British Museum as I was going in."

"Then they know what is on the second scroll as well."

"That would be a logical assumption."

Rhoades could see Al-Bayati's mind working out what he was going to do.

"Where do these people work?"

"They seem to have a special relationship with the American president. The group is run by a woman."

Al-Bayati made a sound of contempt.

Rhoades ignored it. "They have a secure compound outside of Washington, across the river in Virginia."

"Vulnerable?"

Rhoades could see where this was going. "No."

"They could be a real problem for us. I want you to eliminate them."

"That isn't a good idea," Rhoades said, "even if it were possible. The Americans would never stop until they found out who was responsible. Then they would eliminate the threat."

"They won't find out if you do your job properly."

"You pay me to handle things for you. You need to trust me on this. It might be possible to eliminate one or two of them if they were outside the compound. A few deaths would send an appropriate message and it would divert their attention from the scrolls. They'll be busy running around trying to figure out who did it. It would give us time to recover the treasure."

"The ring," Al-Bayati said. "With the ring no one can stand against me. All right, we'll try it your way. Kill as many of them as you can."

Madness, Rhoades thought.

CHAPTER 20

The early morning briefing was in Elizabeth's office, as usual. The day's heat had not yet settled in and Elizabeth had the patio doors open to a light breeze that brought the scent of fresh cut grass and flowers.

"The Israelis want to know what we know about the scroll," she began. "Langley has made us the point on this. It's up to us what we tell them."

"I don't like playing front man for Langley," Nick said. "They wouldn't pass this along unless they thought it might blow up in their faces."

"You may be right, however there's nothing I can do about it. The president has told me to handle it."

"What are you going to tell the Israelis?"

"What we found out. They have the same information as we do about Caprini's scroll."

"And the one in the British Museum?"

"They don't know about that. I thought I'd wait until we know more about what's going on."

Nick smiled.

"Then they haven't seen the coded part," Selena said.

"No. Stephanie has. She's downstairs working on it right now."

"It has to be something simple," Nick said.

"I hope so." Elizabeth picked up her pen and set it down again. "If it has to be decrypted with a companion writing, we're out of luck."

"Like a book code? I don't think those came in until the fifteenth or sixteenth century," Selena said. "Not until after the invention of the printing press."

"If it can be broken, Steph will do it. Meantime, we're stalled out. With Abidi dead we don't know who ended up with that Semtex."

"There's more than one end-user," Nick said. "It turned up in several of the recent bombings."

"Yes. Probably brokered by Abidi and probably to Hezbollah. Someone who wants Semtex to attack the Israelis isn't going to waste it on an obscure Italian professor in France. It doesn't fit."

"There are a couple of things we haven't asked ourselves," Nick said.

"Such as?"

"How did whoever took the scroll find out about it in the first place? No one knew what was on it until it was x-rayed. Somehow the assassin found out about the scroll between the time it was x-rayed and the time Caprini got on that train. That's only a couple of days. What does that tell us?"

"Someone at the x-ray facility tipped them off," Ronnie said. "Has to be."

"It could have been the technician," Selena said, "the one who was killed. He would have known about it before anyone else."

Elizabeth nodded. "He told someone. Or Caprini did."

"I don't think Caprini would do that. He'd want to keep it under wraps so he could make a big splash with an announcement. It was going to make him famous. I suppose he could have talked about it with the technician while they were working on it."

"Good point. We'll focus on him as the possible contact point with the killer."

"If he's the contact he had to call someone," Nick said. "Can we get his phone records?"

"I'm sure we can." Elizabeth made a note. "I'll give it to Stephanie."

"How about Abidi's phone as well? His calls must be in a database somewhere. NSA has been recording everything in Lebanon for years."

Elizabeth made another note. "Nick, you said there were a couple of things we hadn't asked. What else?"

"Why blow up the train?"

"To kill Caprini."

"There are easier ways to do that. I think it was to make it look like the scroll was destroyed."

"That's a stretch."

"Can you think of a better reason? Nothing was found in the wreckage. The French went over the wreckage with everything they had. There should have been something left behind, fragments, traces, something. I think whoever killed Caprini was trying to keep anyone from finding out the scroll had been stolen."

"Why kill all those people?" Elizabeth asked. "It would be easy enough to just steal it after they killed him."

"I don't think they cared about collateral damage. If everyone thinks the scroll was destroyed in the crash then no one will look for it."

"That's cold, Nick," Ronnie said.

"What makes it worse is that it doesn't make any difference. The bad guys didn't know the x-rays still exist and show what's on it."

Diego spoke up. "The Temple treasure would be enough reason to take the scroll out of circulation."

"Maybe." Nick sounded doubtful. "It's still overkill."

"What about the political angle?" Selena asked. "The body of Solomon is a big deal."

Elizabeth picked up her pen and tapped it on her desk.

"I suppose someone could try to sell the location of the tomb to Israel or the Arabs if they knew where it was. They'd never get away with it. It would be like pasting a target on their head. Diego is probably right. They're after treasure."

"Whoever is behind it is one ruthless son of a bitch," Nick said. "Taking out the train like that."

"I wonder how Stephanie's coming with that code?" Elizabeth said her pen down.

Nick nodded at the door. "Why don't you ask her?"

Stephanie entered the room and sat down.

"Ask me what?"

"About the part of the scroll Selena couldn't read," Elizabeth said. "Is it a code?"

"Yes. It's a variation of an *Atbash*, a classic."

"I've heard of that," Selena said.

"What's an Atbash?" Diego asked.

"It's a substitution code using the letters of the Hebrew alphabet. The simplest form substitutes the last letter of the alphabet for the first, the second to last for the second and so on. Back when the scroll was written it was almost unbreakable. No one would've figured it out."

"You said Hebrew. The scroll is written in Aramaic."

"The principle's the same, whatever the alphabet. In our alphabet A becomes Z, B becomes Y, C becomes X and you keep going like that. The Aramaic complicated things but once I knew what I was looking at it wasn't difficult. Freddie printed it out in English."

"Who's Freddie?" Diego asked.

"My favorite computer," Stephanie said. "He's a Cray XT."

She handed copies of the computer print out to everyone.

"The first and last parts are missing. The scroll is damaged."

Selena read the decoded message.

...water. Enough, praises to God. At dawn we continued south. I grow weary of this journey. Two moons and the Sabbath have passed since we began. This land is harsh and cruel, the people few and ignorant. They live in the high places, fearing their neighbors. They worship spirits and animals, without knowledge of the One God. They decorate themselves with flowers and plants in their hair.

We have been following a wide valley. Cliffs rise high on either side and three columns of rock stand guard, one sharp to pierce the sky. If you seek wisdom, look there for...

"For what?" Nick asked.

"It doesn't say," Stephanie said. "That's where something ate the scroll."

"He'd been traveling for more than two months," Selena said. "Assuming he left from Jerusalem, where would that put him?"

"How far could a caravan get in a day?" Diego asked.

"That depends on the country and what they were using for pack animals," Nick said. "Donkeys or camels. Those are both stubborn animals. They'll only go so far unless you drive them to exhaustion."

"On a good road, flat, you can get about twenty miles out of a donkey in a day," Diego said. "That's pushing it."

"How do you know that?"

"We had donkeys on the farm. The town was about ten miles away. I remember my grandfather saying that when the truck broke down he'd hitch two of them up and take a wagon to town. He said it took him all day to go there and back and that the animals were worn out."

"Ephram wouldn't have had a road like that," Stephanie said.

"I don't think he would've used donkeys," Selena said. "Too many things can go wrong in bad country. Camels would be a better choice. They can go farther without water and they can carry more than a donkey."

"You don't think they had wagons?" Nick asked.

"I doubt it. A caravan track would have been impossible for wagons"

"Okay, camels. How far can they go in a day?"

"I don't know."

Stephanie entered a few keystrokes. The answer appeared on the monitor.

"Looks like a camel can travel about twenty miles a day loaded down."

Nick said, "Let's cut that a little bit and allow for things like rough terrain or unavoidable delays. Say fifteen miles a day, loaded to the max. How far would he have gotten when Ephram wrote that part of the scroll?"

Stephanie tapped her keyboard and a map of Saudi Arabia and surrounding areas popped up on the wall monitor.

"Two moons and a Sabbath is a little over two months. If we assume fifteen miles a day, call it a thousand miles."

She drew a line on the screen that went along the eastern edge of the coastal range of Saudi Arabia. The line ended near the modern city of Abha, in the Haraz Mountains.

"That's almost into Yemen."

"Yemen was where the Queen of Sheba is supposed to have ruled," Selena said. "Back then it was all part of Arabia. This coded fragment pops up right after Ephram mentions her. And he uses the word wisdom again. He wrote that in the other scroll."

" 'If you seek wisdom.' What does that mean?" Nick asked.

"Solomon is called the wise king." Stephanie said. "You all know the story about the wisdom of Solomon. If you substitute the word Solomon for the word wisdom it means to look between those three columns of rock he describes in the scroll. It's a landmark."

Elizabeth had been quiet, listening to her team work through the meaning of the coded message. Now she said, "You think Ephram is telling us where Solomon is buried."

Stephanie nodded. "It's possible. Somewhere in the south of what's now Saudi Arabia, right in the middle of those three columns. We find those, we find Solomon."

"Seems too easy," Nick said. "Think about it. Here's this guy who's gone to a lot of trouble to get Solomon and the treasure out of Jerusalem before the Romans get there. He spends two months traveling into Arabia. He decides that's far enough and buries Solomon and the loot right in the middle of a distinctive landmark. Then he writes it down. He leaves a trail a mile wide. Why?"

"The Romans would have had people who could crack a code written in Aramaic," Selena said. "Ephram must have known that sooner or later they'd catch him."

"Exactly," Nick said. "He had to consider that possibility. Remember, the scroll was found in a library that belonged to a Roman. Why make it easy for the Romans to find out where he'd hidden everything if he was captured?"

"Why write it down in the first place?" Ronnie asked.

"In case he got captured or was killed," Nick said. "He wanted to make sure there was some way everything could be recovered in the future."

"I suppose that makes sense," Elizabeth said. "We know Ephram was caught and executed. He was probably tortured. If the Romans did read the scroll they would've sent someone to look for the treasure. I wonder if there's any record of a Roman expedition into Arabia about then?"

"I thought of that," Stephanie said. "I couldn't find anything at all. Even if I had, it wouldn't necessarily mean they were looking for Solomon."

"Has there ever been any record of the Temple treasure being found?" Nick asked.

"No."

"Then there's a good chance it's still out there somewhere."

"If we get an idea where that might be you can verify that for yourself," Elizabeth said.

CHAPTER 21

Everyone liked Chinese food and occasional meals at the Happy Family Chinese restaurant were a chance to unwind and socialize outside of work. Stephanie's car was in the shop. Lucas had come to pick her up. Elizabeth usually went with them. Tonight she'd begged off to catch up on work. Stephanie was trying to persuade her to come.

"You know you want to," Steph said. "Come on. A couple of hours, that's all. Lucas will drive you back."

"I can't, Steph," Elizabeth said. "This report has to go to the White House tomorrow."

"Hey Steph," Ronnie called. "Let's go."

"Go and enjoy yourself," Elizabeth said. "Have an egg roll for me."

Outside, Stephanie got into Lucas's Audi. Nick, Selena, Ronnie and Diego climbed into Ronnie's Hummer. It was a humid July night, last light fading under a darkening sky. Flickers of lightning sent jagged streaks of light across banks of ominous dark clouds building overhead.

"Gonna rain," Ronnie said.

"Soon, I think," Selena said. "Smell the air?"

"We can use it."

They followed Lucas out of the compound and onto the highway, headed for Alexandria.

On the side of the road a man sitting in a gray sedan spoke into his radio as the cars went by.

"On their way. Two cars, a dark blue Audi in front and a black Hummer right behind them. Hell, they might all be in there. I can't tell. They got tinted windows."

"Just the two cars?"

"You think I can't count? Yeah, two. They should come up to you in about three minutes."

"Come join the party."

The man in the gray sedan started his car and pulled out onto the highway.

Ahead, traffic was heavy. Lucas reached over and turned on the radio. Soft jazz filled the comfortable interior of the car.

"How's Junior doing," he said.

"Junioress is just fine," Stephanie said.

The sex of their child was an ongoing joke between them. The truth was that they really didn't care if it was a boy or a girl.

Lucas looked over at Stephanie and thought he'd never have believed he could be this lucky.

The first spray of bullets took out the windshield and the passenger side window. The car filled with pieces of flying glass. Stephanie screamed as the glass exploded. Lucas felt something rip into the side of his face. Instinct kicked in and he swerved left, away from the bullets. More struck the car with dull metallic sounds as he wrenched the wheel over. A harsh burning pain smashed into his shoulder. A tire blew. The car shot across the middle of the road and slammed into an oncoming SUV. In seconds, traffic on the other side of the highway turned to chaos in a snarling pile up of metal and glass.

"Holy shit!" Diego said.

"There," Selena said. She pointed. "On the right. That white van." Two men stood next to the van, holding AK-47s.

Ronnie's Hummer was modified with armor and a heavy grill welded onto the front. The glass was inch-thick and bulletproof against everything except a .50 caliber round. The engine had been modified far past stock. The Hummer was basically a fast tank. In this case it made a good battering ram. Ronnie cut the wheel over, floored the gas and drove straight at the van.

The assassins saw the black machine bearing down on them, swung the guns and began firing on full auto. The windshield starred in a dozen places. The 7.62 rounds weren't powerful enough to break through.

The Hummer plowed into the van and drove it off the side of the road. Ronnie kept his foot down until the van tipped over into an irrigation canal running by the side of the highway. It landed on its side, wheels spinning. Ronnie backed away and stopped. Nick and Diego were out of the car before it stopped moving, pistols drawn.

The two shooters had gotten out of the way before the van crushed them. They raised their rifles and fired. One man cursed and dropped an empty magazine. He reached for another.

Nick held his Sig straight out and ran toward him, firing fast as he went. Some of the rounds missed. Enough found the mark to send him tumbling into the ditch. From the corner of his eye, Nick saw Diego hit the dirt as bullets ricocheted off the pavement around him. Selena knelt by the Hummer, firing at the white van. Diego rolled, came up and fired at the remaining shooter until the slide locked back on his pistol. The man staggered, clutched his gut and crumpled over, his AK firing into the ground.

"The driver," Nick yelled.

He ejected, reloaded and moved toward the overturned truck. Diego came up on his left. He crouched down and moved to the front of the grill. Nick tried to see into the truck. Then Diego rose up and fired four shots at the shattered windshield of the van. Somebody screamed.

Ronnie had just gotten out of the Hummer when shots sounded behind him and a round whistled past his ear. He turned and saw a gray car bearing down on them. Someone leaned out a window, firing one-handed with an assault rifle. Ronnie crouched into a two handed stance and squeezed off rounds at the oncoming car in a steady rhythm. Holes appeared in the windshield. The car swerved right, sailed over the irrigation ditch and crashed into a field beyond. Steam rose from the radiator. Nobody got out of the car.

Ronnie and Selena came up to Nick.

"Could be more inside the van."

"Check it out," Nick said.

One of the doors in back had sprung open. Ronnie ducked and glanced inside.

"Clear," he said. "One man lying on the passenger side. There's a lot of blood. Looks like he's dead."

In the distance a siren sounded.

Nick said, "Diego, make sure they're all dead. Go through their pockets and take everything you find. Then get over across the highway. Don't talk to anyone except us."

"Copy that."

"Lucas and Steph," Selena said.

She sprinted across the highway toward the wrecked Audi.

Nick holstered his pistol.

On the highway people were getting out of their cars. Wreckage littered the road, twisted bits of metal and broken glass. Nick and Ronnie ran between cars until they reached Selena standing by the Audi, trying to open Stephanie's door. Oil and gasoline pooled on the road under the wreck.

The Audi had stopped with the hood buried in the side of a Cadillac SUV. The windows and windshield were shattered. Lucas was slumped over a deflated airbag, unconscious. There was blood everywhere. Stephanie was lying back against a broken seat. Her face was covered with blood. She was unconscious. Her breathing was harsh.

Fumes from gasoline spreading under the wreck were thick.

"We've got to get them out of there," Nick said. "This whole thing could go up in a second."

"I'll get Lucas," Ronnie said. He went around to the driver's side of the car.

Nick tried Stephanie's door. It was crumpled against the frame.

"It's jammed tight," Selena said.

"Need a hand? Looks like it might be hard to get that door open."

Nick turned. A man wearing a baseball cap who looked like he worked construction for a living stood nearby. He had thick, muscular arms and a chest like a gorilla. A faded globe and anchor tattoo decorated his forearm.

"Yeah, thanks."

"Let's give it a try," the stranger said. He grasped the upright side of the door with two hands and set his feet. "You grab the door through the window."

Nick nodded.

"Now."

The two men pulled. With a torturous sound of protesting metal the door came open.

"Steph," Nick said, "we're here. Don't worry, you'll be all right."

Nick couldn't tell how badly she was hurt. Her eyes fluttered and opened. There was blood on her lips.

"The baby..."

"The baby's fine," Nick said. He had no idea if the baby was fine or not but he wasn't going to say anything different.

"Here." The stranger handed Nick a knife. "For the seatbelt."

Nick cut the belt and handed the knife back. He reached behind Stephanie's back and under her legs and eased her out of the car. She moaned.

"Got you, Steph," he said. "It's okay. You're going to be okay."

He turned to the stranger. "Thanks."

"Glad to help."

Ronnie and Diego came around the wrecked Audi carrying Lucas. Gas spread in a thin flood underfoot. They carried Lucas and Stephanie toward the flashing lights of an ambulance coming up on the shoulder of the highway on the other side. More lights were right behind it. They'd reached Ronnie's Hummer when there was a deep thump that vibrated underfoot and a sudden burst of heat. The night lit with orange light. In seconds, the interior of the Audi was engulfed in flame.

Steph was unconscious again. Blood oozed from cuts on her face and a wound in her chest. There was a whistling sound as she breathed.

Sucking chest wound, Nick thought. *Bad news. She could drown in her own blood.*

Ronnie knelt next to Lucas. He looked up at Nick, his face tight and angry.

"He's hit pretty bad."

It began to rain.

CHAPTER 22

The hospital emergency room at night was like every other city ER Nick had ever seen, and he'd seen plenty of them. The floors were covered with a kind of scuffed, neutral colored composition tile that made it easy for the orderlies to mop up blood and vomit without leaving stains. It looked like there was going to be plenty of mopping to do. Wide glass doors went out to a covered entrance where the ambulances could pull up and unload.

The ER was having a busy night. Nick watched a parade of injuries and cops come through the doors. All of them looked like they needed emergency treatment, including some of the cops.

Elizabeth came through the big doors. She dodged around a parked gurney and headed over to the uncomfortable chairs where Nick and the others sat.

"How bad?"

"They're both in surgery. Lucas took a hard hit in his shoulder," Nick said. "He veered away when the shooting started. It changed the trajectory of the bullets or they'd both be dead."

"Stephanie?"

Nick looked down at the floor and sighed. He looked up again. "There are a lot of superficial cuts on her face and scalp from flying glass. None of that is serious. A round went through her right lung and she lost a lot of blood. They won't tell us anything more than that."

Elizabeth was whiter than usual. "What about the baby?"

"Like I said, they won't tell us anything. I wouldn't hold out a lot of hope."

"There's always hope," Elizabeth said.

"The police gave us a lot of trouble. You're going to be hearing from them and probably the president too. Some civilians were hit by those assholes who shot at us and the cops are wondering if it was us. We only got out of there because of the presidential ID."

"Don't worry about it, I'll take care of the cops. And the president."

Elizabeth sat down.

"What do we know?"

"Not much. The shooters knew where we were coming from and what vehicles we were driving. They must've had someone watching the compound. They had radios. When Lucas came up to where they were waiting, they opened up."

"That's it?"

"I went through their pockets before the cops got there," Diego said. He pulled out a wallet he'd taken from one of the dead men. "This is all there was. The others didn't have anything on them."

"Pros," Nick said. "Except for one."

He opened the wallet and showed it to her. It held twenty new one hundred dollar bills and a New York driver's license under a plastic window. The picture was of a man with a narrow face, receding black hair and close set blue eyes. His ears stuck out from the side of his head like handles.

"Patrick O'Malley. It gives an address in Brooklyn."

"Irish?" Elizabeth said.

"I don't think he's Russian with a name like that."

"I'll get..." She stopped and took a deep breath.

"What were you going to say?" Selena asked.

"I started to say that I'd get Steph to run the ID through Interpol. I'll do it when we get back to the compound. We can trace the bills. That might give us a lead."

"We'll get these bastards," Nick said. "They have no idea what they've started."

They waited. It was three hours later before Ronnie said, "There's a doctor coming."

They stood up as the doctor approached. The man looked tired, as if he'd been up for days.

"Who's in charge?" he asked. His name tag ID'd him as Miller.

"I am," Elizabeth said. "You can talk in front of all of us."

Doctor Miller looked at the group and at the holstered guns.

"Are you police?"

"Something like that," Elizabeth said. "Stephanie works for me and she's our friend. I need to know how she is."

"Are you a relative?"

"Doctor Miller, I work for the president. I suggest you tell me immediately how she is."

Harker's tone left no room for argument

Miller looked at his clipboard.

"The bullet entered the right thoracic cavity slightly posterior and lateral to the middle lung, causing internal bleeding and collapse before exiting through the front of the chest wall under the breast. The internal damage was extensive. We've managed to repair it. You got her here in time. Another half an hour and she wouldn't have made it. She's in intensive care."

"She'll be all right?"

"Barring complications, yes. She's a healthy young woman. She won't be running a marathon anytime soon, but in a couple of months she should be fine."

"What about the baby?" Selena asked.

He shook his head. "I'm sorry. The hydrostatic shock was too much for the fetus. She had a miscarriage. If there's any good news in this, she can have another. Assuming there are no further complications. Best not to worry about it."

"What about Lucas?"

"That was close. The bullet that hit him nicked the subclavian artery. He almost bled to death. It missed everything else that was vital and shattered the shoulder joint and clavicle as it exited out the front. There are bone fragments and a lot of tissue damage. He won't be using that arm for quite a while. He's sedated and in recovery."

An announcement paged Miller.

"I'm sorry, I have to go. If there's nothing else..."

"Thank you, Doctor," Elizabeth said.

After Miller was gone they sat down again.

"Best not to worry about it," Selena said. "Easy for him to say."

"Stephanie will be all right," Nick said. "That's the most important thing."

"It might not be to Stephanie."

"One of us should stay with her," Elizabeth said.

Nick looked at her. There were deep shadows under her eyes and lines of strain etched into her pale face.

"We'll set up shifts," he said. "Everybody needs sleep. It's not going to do any good if we're all too tired to find out who came after us."

"I called Langley. Hood is going to post guards," Elizabeth said. "We can't do it by ourselves and whoever is behind this might try again. One of us should still be here for them."

"I'll take the first shift," Ronnie said. "Let's do a four hour rotation."

"Okay." Nick looked at his watch. "It's pushing midnight now. I'll relieve you at four. Selena, you take eight to noon and Diego noon to four in the afternoon. Then we'll do it all over again."

"You left me out of the rotation," Elizabeth said.

"You need sleep, Director. It would be better for you to come and go as you please. You've got damage control. You can get Interpol on our Irish shooter. "

"What about Lucas?" Ronnie said.

"They'll move him to a room once he's out of recovery."

"I'll see if I can arrange for them to be in the same room once Steph is out of the ICU," Elizabeth said.

"Whoever is on shift can look in on him once in a while. Tell him what's going on when he wakes up. I know Lucas. He's going to be pissed. The main problem will be keeping him in bed."

"I wonder if this has anything to do with what happened in Lebanon?" Selena said. "But that doesn't make sense. Why would someone come after us for taking out a lowlife like Abidi?"

"I don't think they would," Elizabeth said, "unless it's about the scroll. Then they might."

"Whoever they are, they're going to regret it," Nick said.

CHAPTER 23

Nick sat in a chair outside Stephanie's cubicle in ICU. Hood had sent over two men from Langley. One now stood guard outside the unit. The other was assigned to Lucas.

Nick could see Stephanie through a large glass window, hooked up to monitors with moving digital readouts. An IV dripped clear fluid into one of her arms. Her face was marked with bandages and orange antiseptic. They'd shaved part of her hair away from her forehead.

Each time he looked at her fed his anger. Someone was going to pay for this.

A nurse came up to him, pretty. She was small like Harker, with curly blonde hair. A name badge identified her as Lois.

"Mister Monroe is out of recovery and awake if you'd like to speak with him. They've moved him to room 332."

Lois looked through the window at Stephanie.

"She's not going to be conscious for quite a while. You should get some rest after you see your friend."

"Thank you."

Nick stood and felt fatigue embrace him, like an insidious lover.

"332 you said?"

"That's right. Take a left when you go out the doors. The elevator is on the right about halfway down the corridor. When you get to the third floor go past the nurse's station and 332 is on the right."

"Thank you," Nick said again.

The elevator was stainless steel and big enough to hold a gurney with a body on it. It rose with silent efficiency. On the third floor Nick turned left past the nurse's station. There was no one there. A man sat down the hall, watching him approach. He stood as Nick came closer. Nick flashed his ID at Langley's man and went in.

Lucas was propped up in bed, his right arm immobilized. Both his eyes were blackened from the airbag. Like Stephanie, an IV fed something into his veins. Unlike Stephanie, he was awake and angry.

"Nick." Lucas cleared his throat. His voice was weak.

"How are you doing?"

"I've been better. What do you know about Steph?"

"She's stable. They've got her sedated in ICU. She's going to be okay. What did they tell you?"

"About the same, along with details about the surgery. She lost the baby."

"I'm sorry, Lucas."

"Damn it, Nick, what the hell happened? Did you get the bastards?"

"They're all dead, Lucas. One of them had ID on him. Harker is following that up. We'll find out who sent them and when we do, we're going to drop the hammer on them."

"They might've been targeting me," Lucas said.

"I don't think so. It doesn't feel right. Why wait until you were over at our compound to go after you, if you were the target? There are easier ways to get at you. I think they wanted to send a message to us. You were in the wrong place at the wrong time."

"Hood isn't going to be happy to have his new DCO out of commission," Lucas said.

"I'm counting on it," Nick said. "We're going to need Langley's resources on this one. Besides, you're not out of commission. You won't be writing any reports for a while. That's what you've got secretaries for. A few days, you'll be back in the office."

"It depends on how Steph is doing."

"Sure. Hood is a decent guy. He's not going to give you a hard time about it. Right now it looks like she's going to be fine."

"They won't let me go see her."

"Lucas, somebody just tried to kill you and did a pretty good job on your shoulder. It's too soon for you to be running around. She's in good hands. When they move her out of ICU, they'll bring her in here. She'll be fine, believe me."

"Yeah. But the bastards who put her in here won't be, once I find out who they are."

You can take that to the bank, Nick thought.

CHAPTER 24

Outside Elizabeth's office the sun was shining. A large orange cat snored in a patch of sun coming through the French doors leading onto the patio.

"That cat makes a lot of noise," Diego said.

"You hear him burp yet?" Ronnie asked.

"Burp?"

"Why do you think we call him Burps?"

"I never thought about it. He's a cat. I don't think about stuff like that."

"Then you have something to look forward to. Ask Nick to tell you about it sometime."

Elizabeth tapped her pen on her desk to get their attention.

"I talked to Steph a little while ago," she said. "She's out of danger."

"That's good news," Selena said.

"Lucas is already talking about getting back to work," Nick said. "A little thing like an AK round isn't going to keep him down for long."

Elizabeth said, "Interpol had a file on Patrick O'Malley."

"They can write closed on it now." Nick looked at her. "Tell me it's got something we can use."

"We do have something."

Elizabeth entered a command on her keyboard. A picture of a castle in Spain came up on the monitor.

"Damn," she muttered. "That's my screensaver. That's not what I was looking for. I wish Stephanie was here."

She tapped the keys and a prison mug shot of Patrick O'Malley appeared. Elizabeth scrolled down to his record.

"A mercenary," Nick said. "It figures."

"A hired gun from Ireland. He's on almost everyone's watch list as an undesirable. He did time in Dartmoor for aggravated assault."

"Sounds like a real winner," Selena said.

"The money in his wallet came through a bank in New York. A direct deposit was wired from abroad into his account. Guess where it came from?"

"Not Lebanon?"

"Straight from Beirut."

"Then this must be about that scroll."

Elizabeth nodded. "Nothing else makes sense."

"Not a smart move," Nick said. "They should have left well enough alone. We were at a dead end. I'm not so sure it was about the scroll. We could have been after Abidi for something that had nothing to do with the scroll. An arms deal, for example."

"How could they know who we are?" Selena asked.

"There were cameras in the nightclub," Diego said. "Someone could have gotten an ID on us from those."

"Selena, maybe," Elizabeth said. "Not you. You're too new."

"I'm not even officially part of the group."

"Do you want to be?" Elizabeth asked. "Now's as good a time as any to get that out of the way."

"When they seconded me to you, I thought you guys were just a bunch of civilians. Would I still be in the Army?"

"No," Harker said. "You'll be honorably discharged with all benefits and receive the same compensation as the others. You'll find it's quite a step up from a sergeant's pay. Nick will be your commanding officer in the field."

"The Army is my career," Diego said.

"You can go back to your unit and your involvement with us ends now. If you say yes and everyone agrees, this will be your new career."

Diego looked at her.

"Diego, things are getting complicated. We have to make plans and I need to know if you want in or out. Yes or no?"

Nick watched him. What would he decide?

"What the hell. Yes."

She looked at the others "Raise your hand if he's in."

All the hands went up.

"Welcome to the team, Boot," Nick said.

"All right. Let's move on," Elizabeth said. "Diego has a point. The only way someone in Beirut would know who we were is from what happened in the club. Who has the ability to identify Selena and make the connection to us? That would take familiarity with the intelligence world we live in. Who has that kind of knowledge?"

"More people than we can identify," Nick said.

"I saw something when you ran that Interpol file," Selena said. She pointed at the monitor where the file was displayed. "Scroll back up a little. It might not mean anything."

They watched the screen as Elizabeth scrolled up.

"There. That paragraph, the one about trying to get O'Malley to turn informer."

The paragraph was only a few sentences long. MI6 had interrogated O'Malley while he was in prison about his association with a known terrorist. The interrogation produced nothing of value.

"You think MI6 is the connection?" Elizabeth asked.

"Not the organization," Selena said. "I was thinking of whoever it was that interviewed him. It's a link between an intelligence connection and the ambush, the only one we've got. Someone from MI6 would know how to find out who we were."

"We need to know who talked to O'Malley," Nick said.

"Lucas could help." Elizabeth drummed her fingers on her desktop. "He's got the resources at Langley. I can't coax information out of our computers like Stephanie can."

"You give Lucas a lead, he'll run with it," Ronnie said.

"It's exactly what he needs," Nick said. "He can help us get these people. He's beating himself up because he didn't spot the ambush."

"No one could've spotted it. There wasn't any reason to expect it. It was just another truck on the side of the road."

"Yeah, but he thinks it's his fault Steph got hurt. This will help him get through it."

"You're turning into a shrink, Nick," Selena said.

"Being around you, I've had a lot of practice."

"I'm not sure how I'm supposed to take that."

Ronnie laughed.

CHAPTER 25

Addison Rhoades didn't know what was going to happen when he entered Al-Bayati's study. After the fiasco in America, his position was in danger. Al-Bayati didn't like mistakes. It made no difference that Rhoades hadn't been on the scene. He'd hired the team that had failed, so he was responsible. Just in case Al-Bayati lost control Rhoades had a Walther PPK tucked away at the small of his back, a favorite of the police since the early days of Hitler's Germany. A classic old school pistol, small, efficient and deadly. One .380 caliber round was enough to stop most people. With Al-Bayati, Addison thought it might take three or four. The pistol had served him well in the past. The hard metal pressing against the small of his back gave him comfort.

To his surprise, Al-Bayati was smiling.

"I have found the tomb," he said.

Rhoades forced himself to seem relaxed.

"You have? That's fabulous, Nazar. Where is it? How did you find it?"

"The second scroll that you retrieved in London contained a coded passage describing the location of the tomb. It's in Saudi Arabia, not far from Yemen."

"You know exactly where it is?"

"It's in an isolated location in the Habala Valley of Saudi Arabia, near Abha. The landmark described is distinctive. There's only one place like that in the country."

"That whole area is considered sensitive by the Saudis," Rhoades said. "The monarchy is worried about troublemakers out of Yemen. It's not going to be easy to get to."

"I have connections there. I can get us in."

"Us?"

"Do you think I would pass up the moment when the tomb is opened? I will be the first to enter."

"As you wish," Rhoades said.

"Yes. Prepare a team. Enough to transport whatever we find."

"We'll need equipment, weapons, vehicles."

"Make a list of what you need. Have it waiting for us when we arrive." Al-Bayati paused. "You did well in London. You failed in America. You had better hope the Americans are unable to connect you to what happened."

"The men I picked were professional, the best in the business. The Americans were lucky. They'll never make the connection."

"That may be," Al-Bayati said. "Do not fail me again. Go. Make the arrangements. I want to leave in three days."

He waved his hand at Rhoades as if he were shooing away a fly.

Rhoades felt the Walther next to his spine, warm from his body and hard against his skin.

I'll kill him, the arrogant bastard. After we find the tomb and the gold.

As he left the room, Rhoades thought about the Americans. He hadn't been lying when he said they'd been lucky. He still didn't understand how they'd escaped. Instinct, perhaps, the instinct of the hunter who knew when he'd become the prey.

Whatever the reason, there was no way they'd find their way back to him.

He turned his mind to the new task Al-Bayati had given him. Rhoades had spent time in Yemen before the fundamentalists had gained so much power. Before his career with British intelligence had gone down the tube.

The thought made him feel as though someone had wrapped his head with steel bands. He forced himself to stop and take a few breaths, to calm the flood of anger that had begun in Al-Bayati's study. His career had been ended by hypocrites. They'd supported his illegal methods, used what he'd gotten from the prisoners he interrogated to further their advancement and then pretended not to know how the information was discovered. Sometimes Rhoades fantasized about returning to England and walking into one of their exclusive meetings with enough firepower to obliterate every one of them.

Fantasy, to think about killing the key players in British government and intelligence. Al-Bayati was a different story. No government would care enough to go looking for the man who killed him. As for friends who might seek revenge, Al-Bayati had none. Business associates would see an opportunity, not a loss. Even the Iranians would simply move on.

When Rhoades left the Habala Valley there would be one more body in Solomon's tomb.

CHAPTER 26

Lucas Monroe had fallen in love with Stephanie the second time he saw her. The first time, he'd been attracted to her easy smile and her obvious comfort with him. Like all black Americans, his radar was tuned to a fine pitch for any sign of racism. As far as he could tell Steph didn't have a racist bone in her body. When she'd gotten pregnant Lucas thought that the gods must be smiling on him. He was in his 40s and had long ago given up ideas of children and fatherhood. Now that he was past the dangerous covert work that had formed most of his career at Langley he had begun thinking about leading a normal lifestyle. The loss of the baby angered him to the core.

They could have another child. Seeing Stephanie grieving hurt him more than anything he could have imagined. She would get over it, if that was the right phrase, as much as he would. He knew no one ever really got over a loss like that. The event would fade, the pain would retreat. Still, there would always be something there. The fact that it had happened because of who they worked for didn't make it any easier.

If there was any consolation, it was that his occupation might provide a way to track down the people responsible. For Lucas, revenge was not a dirty word. He had set the relentless resources of Langley to work on the problem, confident that sooner or later whoever was behind the attack would be identified. Then they would pay. It didn't take long to find something

He called Elizabeth.

"I got what you wanted about O'Malley."

"Are you back at work?"

"Not officially. I can do some things. I called in a favor at MI6. O'Malley was interrogated by an agent named Rhoades. He was kicked out of the service three years ago."

"That gives him the right character recommendation," Elizabeth said.

"What's more interesting is the money trail," Lucas said. "The wire to O'Malley's bank came from a corporate account that launders money for a string of false corporations. They're controlled by a man we've been watching for a long time. His name is Al-Bayati. What I don't know is why Bayati would send a hit team after either of us. "

Bingo, Elizabeth thought.

"I think it's about that scroll."

"Why?"

"You know about Yusuf Abidi and what happened in Lebanon?"

"Yes."

"Nick tailed Abidi to Bayati's villa. I think Abidi sold Semtex to Al-Bayati and that Al-Bayati sent someone to take the scroll, then blew up that train to cover his tracks. I'd put my money on him for the murder at the British Museum and the theft of the other scroll."

"I wouldn't take that bet," Lucas said. "Do you really think he'd go to these extremes on the chance he could find a lost tomb that might not even exist?"

"It's not just any tomb," Elizabeth said. "What would the Israelis do to get back the body of Solomon and whatever was taken from the Temple? What would the Arabs do to stop them? Al-Bayati deals in information. What would the location of the tomb be worth? And don't forget that the Temple contained priceless treasures of gold."

"It still seems far-fetched to me," Lucas said. "Like searching for Atlantis."

"We have a dead shooter who is a direct connection to Beirut and Al-Bayati. It's too much of a coincidence. The attack took place not long after we were in Lebanon, trying to piece together who was responsible for stealing the scroll. Al-Bayati doesn't know that Abidi died before he could tell us anything. I think he set up the hit to keep us from finding out what he was doing."

"Then he should've done a better job," Lucas said. His voice was tight and angry.

"Yes. He's made a mistake by targeting us. I'm sorry you and Steph got caught up in this. I'm sure his men were after us. They couldn't have known who was in the cars."

"What else can I do to help?"

"Send someone over with a high enough clearance to work with me on the computers while Stephanie is recovering. I can't call you every time I need something."

"Let me think about it. A couple of people come to mind. I'll talk to Hood about lending you someone. I don't think it's a problem."

"How's the shoulder?" Elizabeth asked.

"Hurts like hell. The painkillers help some."

"Stephanie?"

Elizabeth heard Lucas sigh. "She thinks about the baby all the time. She cries a lot. And she's pissed, really pissed."

"That's a lot better than feeling sorry for herself."

"When she's not talking about stringing up the people who did this or staring out the window she spends most of her time reading romance novels. Right now she's reading a book about a woman who travels back in time to 18th-century Scotland and gets involved with pirates."

"Every good romance novel has a pirate," Elizabeth said.

"I'll get someone over there to give you a hand. Keep me posted on what you find."

"You know I will. Thanks, Lucas."

After she'd hung up, Elizabeth thought about the conversation. *Al-Bayati*. Her intuition had been right. Now that she had a clear focus, she could begin planning how to bring him down. Before that happened she needed to be positive he was the one behind the attacks. The proof she needed was out there, she was certain. When she found it she wasn't going to stop until Al-Bayati was finished.

CHAPTER 27

The next morning Elizabeth got a call from security at the entrance to the compound.

"Director, I have someone here who says he's from Langley and that DCO Munroe sent him over. Should I let him in?"

"He has identification?"

"Yes ma'am, CIA."

"Send him in."

Elizabeth went to the front door and waited. A white Ford pulled up and parked. The man who got out was slight and round shouldered, with curly black hair and glasses. He wore a rumpled blue suit and a tie with a tiny knot that looked like it would have been the height of fashion in 1950. He reached inside the car and took out a brown leather case. As he stepped onto the porch Elizabeth opened the door for him.

"Are you Director Harker? I'm Joe Eggleston. The DCO said you need some help with computers?"

"What did he tell you about us?"

Elizabeth led Eggleston inside and closed the door. They went into her office.

"Not much. Only that I should get over here and help you any way I can. He said everything you do is classified. I have the clearance to look at whatever you've got."

"Good. You'll be filling in for my deputy until she returns."

Eggleston walked over to a laptop sitting on Elizabeth's desk.

"Is this what's giving you trouble?"

"Not exactly," Elizabeth said. "Come with me."

She took Eggleston downstairs. The muffled sounds of gunshots came from behind the closed door of the indoor range. Eggleston looked surprised.

"You have a shooting range?"

"Among other things. This way."

She led him past the ops center and the swimming pool to the computer room.

In an earlier life, the computer room had been a hardened magazine for Nike missiles. Now it housed a row of Cray computers and the communications gear that let Elizabeth communicate with her team in the field. A console with three monitors sat at one end of the room, next to the Cray XT Stephanie called Freddie. An empty coffee mug with a wolf on it sat on the console. The room smelled faintly of ozone. It was cold.

Eggleston shivered.

"This is what you'll be working with."

"Whoa," he said. "Not a laptop."

"No."

"I'll need the password."

"I thought you might. I talked to Stephanie earlier. Look on the bottom of the mug."

Eggleston walked to the console and picked up the cup. He turned it over. Taped to the bottom was a small piece of white paper with a long string of characters and numbers.

"There are some files you can't access that are eyes only for myself and Stephanie. What I need you to do is begin searching for pieces of information and people I want to know more about."

"I can be up and running pretty quick," Eggleston said.

"Take your time. Stephanie has got this set up exactly the way she wants it, so please don't change anything. I think you'll find you don't need to. She's very thorough."

"If she set this up and programmed it, I want to meet this lady," Eggleston said.

He ran his fingers along the edge of the console and looked at the computers.

Elizabeth saw that he was hooked. It was the kind of look she'd seen Stephanie get from time to time, as if she was in the presence of an all-knowing entity that could tell her anything she wanted to know.

"Get familiar with everything. Do you think you can run the communications gear?"

Eggleston looked at the array. "No problem. I've had a radio license since I was eleven. This is nice stuff. It will be easy to work with."

"Excellent."

Eggleston gestured at the console. "What would you like me to do first?"

"There was a recent theft and murder at the British Museum. I want you to access the CCTV recordings at the Museum and cross-reference them with our database of known undesirables. It's possible someone we recognize will turn up. Can you handle that?"

"Hack into the British Museum?"

"Yes."

"What about legal issues?"

"What do you mean?"

"You know, accessing confidential information in another country."

"Are you sure you work at Langley?" Elizabeth said.

"Just asking," Eggleston said.

"There's a coffee maker over there. The bathroom is in the ops center."

"Ops center?"

"The big room we passed near the pool. If you run into any of the others on the team, introduce yourself. Any other questions?"

"I don't think so. If I come up with something, I'll ask."

"Then I'll leave you to it."

Back upstairs, Elizabeth poured a cup of coffee and sat down at her desk. She missed Stephanie. Eggleston would have to do until Steph came back. At least he seemed to know what he was doing.

By late afternoon, he'd proved it.

CHAPTER 28

Eggleston sat apart from the others at the morning briefing. He'd been a little intimidated at first. They all had guns, even the women.

Who are these people? The security here is as good as Langley's, except the place looks like somebody's house in the country. The kind of place where the owner is probably out on a golf course somewhere, hitting a few balls.

They'd been polite, keeping their distance. It didn't bother him. He was used to being an outsider. The truth was that he preferred his cubicle at Langley and his computers to interacting with his peers and the rest of the world. For Joe Eggleston, heaven was a comfortable chair and a console hooked into the biggest computer he could find. This temporary assignment to Harker's group was the closest thing to heaven he'd found in a long time.

"You've all met Joe," Elizabeth said. "I asked him to look at surveillance tapes from the British Museum on the day of the murder. Joe, show them what you found."

Eggleston tapped a key on his laptop. A black and white picture of the front of the Museum appeared on the wall monitor. It showed Selena and Nick starting to leave the building.

"You guys look like tourists," Diego said.

"That's kind of the point," Nick said. "How do you think we should look?"

"I don't know. James Bond never looks like a tourist."

"James Bond is a character in a movie."

"Yeah, but you gotta set a standard somewhere."

Elizabeth rapped her pen on the desk. "That's enough. Let's focus."

"Sorry," Diego said.

Eggleston was shocked. Comments like that at a high level briefing at Langley would have gotten somebody in real trouble.

The picture changed and began rolling in real time. Nick and Selena started down the steps. A tall, lanky man walked past them going the other way. As he passed, he turned and looked at Selena. Eggleston froze the video. The man's face was fully visible.

"This man's name is Addison Rhoades," Elizabeth said. "He's the one who interrogated O'Malley at the prison. He used to work for MI6. Now he works for Nazar Al-Bayati."

"You think he's the one who killed Sir Peter?" Selena asked.

"I do."

"What about tapes inside the building? Do they show anything?"

"The coverage is minimal. The only extensive coverage is in sections where valuables like gold and jewelry are displayed. Rhoades avoided the cameras. There was no camera in the storage room where the scroll was kept and where Sir Peter was killed. You don't see Rhoades again until he comes out. There's no sign of the scroll but that doesn't mean anything. It would be easy enough to hide it under his coat."

Nick said, "Rhoades knew O'Malley and works for Al-Bayati?"

"That's right."

"And you think Abidi sold Semtex to Al-Bayati, who used it to cover his tracks after stealing the scroll in France."

"Right."

"Tell me if I've got this figured out." Nick ticked off points on his fingers. "We go looking for Abidi to ask him about the Semtex. He dies. Al-Bayati gets nervous about what he might have told us and tells Rhoades to find out who went after him. Rhoades uses his connections to ID Selena and Al-Bayati tells Rhoades to get us out of the way. He sends a hit team that includes O'Malley. They're after us. Steph and Lucas get caught in the crossfire. That about it, Director?"

"That's what I think."

"Son of a bitch," Nick said. "What are we going to do about it?"

"I want you to go back to Lebanon and have a heart-to-heart talk with Al-Bayati. Recover the scrolls if you can. That's not a priority."

"I don't think we can take Bayati at his house, Director," Ronnie said. "You asked us to check it out. Diego and I looked at the satellite shots for a long time and thought it through, how we'd do it. We both think it's a high failure mission."

Diego nodded his head in agreement.

Nick scratched his head. "We've taken walled compounds before."

"Not like this one," Ronnie said. "This one has all the bells and whistles. There are rolls of razor wire on top of the wall. It's electrified and I'll bet it's alarmed. There are cameras and guards everywhere and the whole place is lit up like Yankee Stadium at night. We'd have to go up the cliff on the water side to avoid being seen and there's more wire at the top. Once we're in the compound there are a couple of dozen men to go through before we make it to the house. Every one of them carries an AK. The gate would take a tank to break through it."

"Okay. Then we'll get him when he's not in the villa."

"That's a problem," Elizabeth said. "He almost never leaves his villa."

"We could wait."

"You might wait a long time."

"Everyone can be gotten to, sooner or later. There has to be a way."

Selena had been quiet. Now she said, "We're mad about what happened to Stephanie. It won't do her or us any good to go after Al-Bayati if it gets us killed. Suppose we did get into the compound? What then? What would we gain by that?"

"What are you getting at?" Elizabeth asked.

"It's not as though we have to retrieve the scrolls. We know what's on them and we can assume Al-Bayati does too. He's gone to a lot of trouble to get his hands on them. He's after the treasure, if it can be found. The second scroll tells everybody where it is. What would you do if you were him?"

"Go after it," Diego said.

Selena nodded. "Right. We should be patient. Put a satellite or a drone on him. Wait for him to make his move. If I were him, I'd make it soon. Once he's out of his compound we can get him."

"He might just send a team," Elizabeth said.

"I don't think so. He wants to find that tomb. I don't think his ego would let somebody else do it for him. If that gold is there, it's too much of a temptation. Al-Bayati doesn't strike me as the trusting type. He isn't going to let someone else do it for him."

"If he leaves the villa he'll be traveling in an armored vehicle with an escort," Nick said. "It's how I'd do it if I were him. Same problem as the villa. It needs more than we've got to take him down."

"It needs more than we've got if we go after him in Lebanon," Selena said. "Not in the Habala Valley. Not unless he's got a military escort."

"Al-Bayati's dealings with Tehran have made him unpopular with the Saudis," Elizabeth said. "He's not going to be welcome. He'll make it as low-profile as he can."

"He's got millions. Money buys a lot of low-profile," Nick said. "It can get him in and out of the country without much of a problem."

"So we wait?" Selena asked.

"Until we have a clean shot at him," Elizabeth said. "Meanwhile I want you to go find that tomb. I asked Joe to try and locate those three pillars mentioned in the scroll. Joe?"

"These are satellite shots of the only possibility," Eggleston said.

The pictures on the monitor showed a long valley in an area of low mountains, bounded on both sides by hills and cliffs. Eggleston zoomed in on a hilltop where three columns of stone were visible. One of them was needle shaped, the other two flat on top.

"This is the Habala Valley in southern Saudi Arabia. Those three columns are a well-known landmark in the area."

"Looks deserted," Diego said.

"It is. The nearest town is some distance away. Nobody lives out that way. It's pretty desolate, almost a desert. It's the only thing in Saudi Arabia that fits with the description Director Harker gave me."

"I knew this was coming," Nick said. "It's hot as hell in that part of Saudi Arabia this time of year."

"Then I guess you'd better take a lot of sun block," Elizabeth said. "Put together the mission."

"Getting in could be a problem."

"I'll talk to the president. He'll give us what we need."

"You want us to try and recover anything if it's there?"

"Pictures would be enough. If there's a small object you can take with you, fine. Physical proof is always good."

"How soon do you want us to leave?"

"As soon as you can study the surveillance shots and get your gear together. This won't be the first time we've inserted a team into the kingdom. I can get you there but once you're in country, you're on your own until extraction."

"Some things never change," Ronnie said.

"That's all," Elizabeth said.

Eggleston waited until the others had gone.

"Director, have you got a couple minutes to bring me up to speed on what's happening here? It would help if I knew more about the situation."

"Sorry, Joe, there hasn't been time to fill you in. You're right, of course."

Elizabeth spent the next ten minutes telling Eggleston what had happened. About the scrolls, Al-Bayati, the nightclub in Lebanon, the attack on the cars that had injured Lucas and put Stephanie in a hospital. The reason she was sending the team to Saudi Arabia.

"That's quite a story," Joe said.

"I'm afraid it's only the beginning. We have to make sure Al-Bayati doesn't loot that tomb, assuming it exists. We won't know if it does unless we check the location given on the scroll for ourselves. If Nick finds the tomb things will get complicated fast. Any relics from the Jewish Temple have to go back to Israel. The same for the body of Solomon if it's there."

"Aren't the Arabs going to have something to say about all this?"

"They'll have plenty to say if they find out about it. So far it doesn't look as if they have. We'll get in and out before they know we're there. If we can verify that the tomb exists, I'll hand the whole thing over to the president and let him worry about it."

"Is this what you do all the time?"

"Pretty much." She paused. "On a high risk mission like this I rely on real-time communication with the team. It's what gives a small unit like us the edge. What I see on the satellites can make the difference between success and failure. It can make the difference between living and dying for them. It's going to be your job to keep that online and functioning as it should. If you're not up to it, I want you to tell me now."

"I can handle it, Director."

Elizabeth looked at him and hoped that he could.

"Very well."

She reached into her desk and took out a sheet of paper.

"I'm told you have an eidetic memory. Is that true?"

"Yes. I never forget anything. Sometimes I wish I could."

She handed him the paper. "This is a list of current access codes for our military and communications satellites. Memorize it now and give it back to me."

She waited while Eggleston scanned the paper. His lips moved silently as he read.

"All right." He handed it back to her.

"What's the code combination on line four?"

Eggleston read it back to her.

"Good. I just wanted to make sure. Set up full surveillance on Al-Bayati's villa in Lebanon. Keep a visual on it 24/7. If you want to use a military unit, tell me and I'll get it authorized. I want to know if Al-Bayati goes anywhere. It shouldn't be hard to spot him. Pull up his files and familiarize yourself with what he looks like."

"Yes, ma'am."

"Director."

"Yes, Director."

"After you cover Al-Bayati program surveillance over the target area in Saudi Arabia. Any other questions?"

"No."

"Once the team is in Saudi Arabia they're at high risk. Nobody's playing games here. If this goes wrong they could all be killed. Don't let me down."

"Don't worry, Director. I can do this."

"Good. Go set up the surveillance."

Eggleston went down to the computer room thinking about what Harker had told him. He was beginning to understand why they all carried weapons.

CHAPTER 29

Major Dov Yosef brushed a speck of dirt from his uniform and cursed the faulty air-conditioning that had turned his office into a sauna. He contemplated a plaque on the wall with the motto and winged sword of the Israeli *Duvdevan*.

כִּי בְתַחְבֻּלוֹת, תַּעֲשֶׂה-לְךָ מִלְחָמָה

"For by wise counsel thou shalt make war."

The quotation was from Proverbs. Once it had been the official motto of The Institute for Intelligence and Special Operations, better known as Mossad. That had been changed to a different proverb reflecting the idea that many counselors were needed. Dov thought it suited the officious bureaucracy of Mossad perfectly. He was of the opinion that the fewer counselors the better, particularly when it was time to mount a mission. As often as not Dov's orders came from Mossad headquarters. Sometimes too many cooks had been stirring the operational soup.

Duvdevan wasn't the official designation of Dov's unit. The word meant cherry, a nickname that reflected the unit's unique position within the Israeli Defense Force. The cherry was the fruit at the top of the tree, just as the Duvdevan was at the top of its particular tree, the most elite of a very tough army's special forces.

Alone within the IDF, the Duvdevan operated independently of other Israeli units. Unit operatives spoke fluent Arabic and often dressed in Arab civilian clothes, blending in with Arab populations. Many of Dov's men spent a lot of time in Gaza. The Duvdevan operated throughout the Arab countries surrounding Israel as well as within its borders. It was a difficult and dangerous job. If an operative was caught, he was a dead man.

Dov's unit had no specific mission except relentless defense and counter attack against the enemies of Israel. Because it was under the Judea and Samaria division of the IDF it could move anywhere within the country without answering to the normal army chain of command. It was the unit of choice for secretive and dangerous counterterrorism missions in the Middle East. Other field units in Israeli intelligence, like the lethal *Kidon*, fanned out across the world to carry out their operations. The Duvdevan stayed close to home.

The heat wasn't the only thing on Dov's mind. He'd just finished reading a report on two ancient scrolls that spelled trouble. He thought of them in his mind as the French scroll and the English one. X-ray pictures of the French scroll and translations of both were part of the report. The primitive code that pointed to the probable location of the tomb of Solomon had been easily broken by Israeli intelligence.

The report speculated that the destruction of the night train to Rome and the explosion in Grenoble were connected to the scroll examined in France. It ended with a promise of further investigation.

Dov had seen reports like that before. Further investigation could mean anything, reveal nothing. In the meantime Dov had been told to plan a mission to find out whether or not the tomb of Solomon and the Temple treasure still existed. It was like being told to find water in the Arabian desert, only worse. There were satellites that could do that. He felt a headache start up.

A knock at the door interrupted his thoughts.

"Come."

Dov's commanding officer came into the room. Dov started to rise.

"Colonel."

"Stay where you are, Dov."

Colonel David Cohen was pushing fifty. He looked as fit as many men half his age. Dov was ten years younger than the Colonel. Even so, he had a hard time keeping up with his superior during their frequent runs together. Dov was tall and lean, bronzed by the desert sun, with a body that was mostly hard muscle. Cohen was shorter, dark and wide. He looked like he should be carrying a short sword with the rebels at Masada in the days of the Roman war. There was something ancient looking about him, as if this current incarnation as a warrior was just one more in a long history.

Dov, on the other hand, was the essence of an officer in a modern army which preferred Tavor assault rifles to swords and spears. His eyes were blue, the result of some unknown European ancestor. His looks were marred by a patchwork of scars where plastic surgery had repaired burns on the side of his face. It gave him a dangerous look. He was a reasonable man except when confronted with someone he believed to be an enemy. For Dov there were many enemies but he reserved special hatred for the Arabs.

Four years before he'd been vacationing with his wife and child at Eilat when an Arab terrorist decided it was time to martyr himself for the cause. Dov had survived. His wife Hannah and his daughter Rebeka had not. As far as the Arabs were concerned, Dov had no interest in either forgiving or forgetting.

"Take a walk with me to the canteen, Dov," Cohen said. "It's too damn hot to be sitting in these offices."

"I could use something cold. Let me secure this."

Dov got up and went to a safe, opened it and placed the report inside. He closed the heavy door and spun the dial.

"That the report on the scrolls?"

"Yes," Dov said.

"This one is going to be tricky."

"They all are."

"We have to follow up on this."

"I don't need to be convinced. If this tomb exists and if it's in Saudi territory, we have to find it before they do."

"The word is out about what that Italian discovered," Cohen said. "I'd be surprised if the Arabs didn't know about it. Certainly the Americans."

"That would be a safe assumption," Dov said. "We should try and find out what they know."

"I put in a request. Relations have been strained with Washington," Cohen said. "I'm not sure if they'll tell us anything. Not that they usually do."

They came to the canteen, went in and ordered iced drinks. They took a seat in the corner, away from the few others in the room.

"Have you had time to think about it yet?" Cohen asked.

"I only got the report an hour ago," Dov said. Cohen waited.

"The murder of the Italian and the explosion in the train. They're obviously related. Then a second scroll taken from the British Museum and another murder. Who did it? Whoever it was has got the scrolls, would you agree?"

"I would."

"I don't know what their agenda is but it can't be any good for us."

"You have any ideas?" Cohen made circles on the table with the condensation from his glass.

"Has anyone analyzed the explosive used on the train?"

"Yes. It was Semtex, manufactured during the Bosnian war. There's plenty of it on the black market. Some of it has been showing up lately in the bombings."

Dov heard *bombings*. Cohen's words blurred with the sound of the ceiling fan over their table. Memory flooded in.

He's walking in the market with Hannah and Rebeka. It's a beautiful day and the market is crowded. People are in a good mood. Rebeka is holding a strawberry ice and trying not to get the melting drops on her new outfit. Music from street musicians floats in the air. Hannah points at a stall selling bolts of cloth.

"I want to look at that one," she says. "The color is perfect for a new tablecloth."

They are standing next to a stall selling small tanks of propane. She looks at him and smiles, her face full of love. They start toward the cloth stall. From the corner of his eye, he sees a man suddenly stand still in the midst of the crowd flowing around him. He's an Arab, out of place in this market. Something sounds an alarm in Dov's mind. It's too late. The man reaches under his robe and everything disappears in flame and heat and noise.

The shockwave knocks him to the ground. The propane tanks nearby erupt in violent flame that scorches over him, over Hannah, over Rebeka, over the crowd. He sees the blistered bodies of his wife and child lying unmoving on the pavement before he fades into unconsciousness.

"Dov? You okay?"

Colonel Cohen's voice brought him back.

"Sorry."

Cohen sighed. "You were remembering, weren't you?"

"Yes. It was when you mentioned the bombings."

"Have you been seeing someone about it?"

"I'm fine, don't worry about it." He shook off the heavy feeling that always accompanied the flashback. "We were talking about the Semtex. Are there any leads on who supplied it?"

Cohen decided to let it go. "Not yet. If there is one, it will turn up." He paused. "You're going to have to look for that tomb."

"Yes, sir. I'll put the mission together."

"I don't need to tell you that the Arabs will shit a brick if they catch you."

"They won't catch us," Dov said. "If they get lucky and do, they'll wish they hadn't."

CHAPTER 30

The modified UH-60 Blackhawk spiriting the team through the night and into the Habala Valley wasn't like any chopper Nick had ever seen. It was a product of the Sikorsky skunk works, funded by DARPA, the Pentagon's secret weapons development program. The exterior shape of the bird resembled a machinist's experiment with origami, flat surfaces covered with dark, molded fabric and set at odd angles to each other. The tail rotor was shrouded in a disk like cover. It was so quiet Nick could forget it was there. He'd never been in a helicopter as quiet as this one. A high-class ride, as choppers went. All that was missing were soft leather seats, drinks and music playing in the background.

Slipping through the Saudi air defenses presented little difficulty. They crossed into the kingdom flying low and fast. The pilot set them down on the valley floor, not far from their objective. They were out of the bird with their gear and on the ground in seconds.

They watched their only connection to home and safety speed off into the darkness, a black shape against a black sky lit with millions of stars. The starlight was bright enough to make out peaks rising on either side of the valley. The mountains weren't much more than three thousand feet high but they were rugged, steep and inhospitable. It was a harsh, sandy land.

It was cold now. When the sun rose the temperature would climb to well over a hundred.

"Lock and load," Nick said.

They were traveling light, rations for three days and six thirty round magazines of ammo, plus four magazines each for their sidearms. Each of them carried an MP-5 chambered for the same .40 caliber round as their pistols. They charged the weapons. The metallic sounds echoed in the still night air.

"Quiet, isn't it," Diego said. "Peaceful."

"Let's hope it stays that way."

Nick activated the satellite comm link. They could all hear what was said.

"Base, this is One."

In Virginia, Elizabeth had been waiting. She heard Nick's voice, loud and clear. Eggleston had done his job.

One less worry, she thought.

"One, copy," she said. "What's your status?"

"Down and good. Moving out now. One, out." Nick signed off.

"It will be light soon." He looked at his GPS and pointed. "That way. Let's go."

He set off at a fast walk. The others strung out behind him, leaving space between. One of the first things Selena had learned in the field with Nick was to avoid bunching up in hostile territory. By now it was second nature to her.

The GPS guided them away from the easy path of the ancient riverbed that formed the valley floor. The ground rose in a steep slope covered with thick clumps of juniper and scattered trees. Above them, the three pillars of rock Ephram had described on the scroll loomed against a predawn sky.

They pushed up the slope. It was hard going, through tough branches and prickly leaves that caught on their clothes and scratched at them. The sun was breaking the horizon in the east when they reached the base of the first pillar.

"It will be full light soon," Nick said. "Let's move in between the rocks."

"Isn't this place some kind of tourist attraction?" Selena asked.

"Not much of one. In the winter, maybe, when it's cooler. I don't think we're going to see any tourists."

"Sure, but the locals must've been through here a lot since that scroll was written," Diego said. "If that tomb is here, how come nobody found it?"

"I don't know. We still have to look for it. Makes sense that any entrance would be so well hidden no one would pay attention if they were looking right at it."

"By now it's probably covered over by these damn bushes," Ronnie said.

They made their way into the center of the three pillars. The formation formed a flat, rough circle dotted with more junipers and trees. There were animal tracks and winding trails in the greenery. In a firefight, the place would be a death trap.

"This sucks," Diego said.

Selena saw something on her sleeve. She made a face and plucked it off. "Ticks. The place is full of ticks."

"Great," Nick said. "Probably venomous spiders as well. Scorpions too. The brown ones will hurt like hell. The black ones will kill you. This is high desert. Make sure you're bloused up good and tight."

"Snakes?" Selena asked. "Are there snakes?"

"Yes. Several poisonous ones, vipers. They're deadly, so watch where you walk or sit. Don't stick your hand where you can't see it."

"Now you tell me. This place must give Hell a run for its money."

"I didn't want to freak you out," Nick said.

"I wouldn't talk if I were you," Selena said. "Spiders and snakes get to you as much as they do me."

"I hate spiders," Diego said.

"They're afraid of people," Ronnie said. "They'll hear us coming and get out of the way."

"Like that big one on your foot?"

"Whaa!"

Ronnie jumped to the side.

Diego started laughing and the others joined in.

"Very funny," Ronnie said. "I'll remember that."

As the sun rose, the morning light revealed a place of desolate beauty. It was already getting hot. The pillars rose tall into the air. They were composed of reddish stone and reminded Nick of Utah.

They found a place near one of the pillars with only a scattering of vegetation and stopped to look around. Outcrops of granite poked through the dry, sand colored ground. There were flat rocks everywhere, perfect hiding places for the deadly wildlife that lived here. The top of the hill would make a great location for a nature special on public television. Nick could have done without it

"How do you want to do it?" Ronnie asked. "Spread out or stay together?"

"I think we should stay together. This place isn't so big that we need to fan out. Keep a few feet apart."

"Do you think Ephram would have buried it?" Selena asked. "It looks like it's solid rock underneath the surface dirt."

"I don't think so," Nick said. "Look for a natural crevice, something they could use to hollow out a hiding place. It's what I'd do. Then I'd seal it up with rocks and dirt. In a year or two you'd never know anyone had ever been here. There weren't many people in this area back then."

Elizabeth's voice crackled through the comm link.

"One, you copy?"

"Copy."

"Al-Bayati is on the move. He boarded a plane in Beirut an hour ago with a flight plan for Yemen. He's headed your way."

"How long till he gets here?"

"Sometime in the afternoon your time. It depends on what he's using for transportation and whether or not he gets hung up at the border."

"He'll have a way to cross or he wouldn't be coming."

"Any luck?"

"Not yet. We're just beginning to look."

"Keep me posted. Out."

"Company coming," Nick said.

"We'll make sure he gets a nice welcome," Ronnie said.

CHAPTER 31

Addison Rhoades leaned back in the comfortable lounge seat of Al-Bayati's private jet and closed his eyes. It had been a while since he'd taken one of the foil wrapped balls. His body hummed and vibrated, out of harmony with the steady pulse of the engines. He felt like a guitar string tuned too tight, ready to snap if plucked. He'd taken a tablet of morphine half an hour before. Now he waited for the drug to kick in and take the edge off the unpleasant sensations.

It was no use, he had to sit up and do something, distract himself. He reached down into his travel bag and took out a cleaning kit. He pulled a Glock GP27 from his shoulder holster and laid it on the coffee table in front of his seat. Along with the Walther PPK the Glock was his favorite pistol, compact and powerful. It was meant for up close and personal, where almost all gunfights with pistols took place. Unloaded it weighed less than 20 ounces. He field stripped the weapon and started to clean it.

The morphine kicked in and his body relaxed. Rhoades took a deep breath and felt his mood improve. The smell of gun oil and cleaner was familiar, the ritual soothing. He'd always liked guns. They were reliable if you took care of them, unlike people. With a good gun you knew what to expect.

They'd land in Yemen near the Saudi border within the hour. Al-Bayati's connections meant no problems with the authorities. Men loyal to Rhoades would be waiting with vehicles at the landing strip.

From there it was a few hours overland to their objective in the Habala Valley.

The tomb of Solomon and Al-Bayati's lunatic dream of a magic ring.

Rhoades didn't care about a ring. He cared about gold. If the tomb was there, Al-Bayati would never leave it. Rhoades had made up his mind that it was time to move on. As soon as they found the gold he would kill Al-Bayati. Until they found it he needed him alive.

He finished cleaning the pistol, reassembled it and placed it back in the holster. He packed the cleaning kit away as the plane began its descent to the barren desert landscape below and an abandoned military airbase close to the Saudi border. Al-Bayati had no intention of flying into Saana and dealing with the Houthi rebels in control of the city. Ten minutes later they were on the ground. A cluster of vehicles waited on the side of the runway.

The sun beat down on Bayati as he stood on the cracked concrete at the foot of the airplane stairs. He wiped his brow with a silk handkerchief.

"Hot," he said. "I'd forgotten how hot this godforsaken place can be."

"With luck we won't be here long," Rhoades said. "Here comes our escort."

Three Land Rovers painted desert tan pulled up by the plane, followed by two Toyota pickup trucks with Russian Kord heavy machine guns mounted in the beds. A third truck was empty, backup for transporting whatever they might find.

The Kord 12.7 mm was a recent addition to Russian infantry armament, replacing the older NSV that had been the staple weapon for years. It featured a higher rate of fire than the NSV. An alloy barrel that increased accuracy and effectiveness up to about 2000 meters. It wasn't a good idea to be on the wrong end of one of them when it was in use.

Al-Bayati appreciated fine weapons. He looked at Rhoades.

"Kords. I'm impressed. You think we'll need them?"

"There's been a lot of rebel activity around here," Rhoades said. "I thought a little extra firepower wouldn't hurt. The men are all experienced and well armed. No one will bother us if they know what's good for them."

Al-Bayati grunted and heaved his bulk into one of the Land Rovers. Rhoades got into the back seat. He took out his GPS, already programmed with the location of the three pillars.

"We'll use the old crossing," he said to the driver. "The one abandoned by the British. You know the one I mean?"

"I know it. Rough road," the driver said.

His name was Jan Vorster. He was a fourth generation Afrikaner, a grizzled former policeman who'd gotten out of the Republic of South Africa when apartheid crumbled. His talent for violence had turned out to be useful in his new role as a mercenary. It paid better, too. Rhoades had met him during an MI6 operation in Darfur. As far as he could tell Vorster was the ideal soldier for hire, a man without bothersome moral considerations or qualms of conscience about what might have to be done.

"Watch out for patrols," Rhoades said.

The six vehicles set out for Saudi Arabia.

CHAPTER 32

On top of the hill it felt like being inside an oven. Rippling waves of heat rose from the rocks and sand. They'd searched for a sign of the tomb and found nothing. Now they were going around the columns once more. Nick had decided that the whole exercise was a waste of time and was ready to concede defeat. Their desert camouflage uniforms were soaked black with sweat. Selena moved with the others around the base of one of the pillars. Suddenly she froze.

"Snake."

Nick looked where she was pointing. The snake was curled up on a flat rock next to the column, within striking distance from where she stood. It was a yellow, sandy color, with a round snout and round cat eyes. Two horns stuck up from its head, giving it a demonic look. It raised its head and looked at her.

"Don't move," Nick said. "That's a horned viper."

He reached for his pistol. Ronnie laid a hand on his arm.

"I'll get it," he said. "Better not to make the noise."

He eased a throwing knife from a sheath strapped under his arm and launched it at the snake. The blade arced through the sunlight and buried itself behind the viper's head. The snake contorted, showing its fangs. Selena backed away.

"Wouldn't be good to get bitten by one of those," Nick said. "It creates serious pain and a lot of damage. We're a long way from medical help for a viper bite."

"Gee, thanks for reminding me."

The snake stopped moving. Ronnie retrieved his knife.

"That was slick," Diego said. "Too bad you had to kill it."

"Selena was too close. It would have struck if she'd moved. Otherwise we could have left it."

Selena stared at the column where the snake had been dozing.

"There's something here."

She pointed at a faint groove in the rock on the edge of a wide, vertical fissure climbing the side of the column. The fissure was hard to see, filled with a thick growth of juniper. There was no way to tell if it went deeper into the column or was simply a wide crack on the surface.

"That mark could be man-made," she said.

"Maybe," Nick said. "What would cause something like that?"

"A rope? I don't know. It just doesn't look natural to me."

"Me neither," Diego said.

They'd passed the spot before and decided it was solid. "We haven't seen anything else," Nick said. "Let's clear away the greenery."

They hacked away at the growth until they could get next to the fissure, then began prying out accumulated dirt and debris. A small opening appeared. A dry, dusty odor drifted out of the blackness.

"I'll be damned," Nick said. "I think we've found it."

The discovery energized them. Another half-hour and they'd cleared away a narrow passage into the column.

Nick turned on his flashlight and aimed it into the dark interior.

"What do you see?" Selena said.

"Someone widened this passage. I can see tool marks on the rock."

"Nothing else?"

"No. We'll have to go inside."

"There could be spiders. More snakes."

"I don't see any webs. Anyway, we don't have a choice. Just watch where you step."

Single file, they followed Nick into the interior. The passage was barely wide enough to let them pass. After a short distance it curved to the right and opened into a large, natural chamber in the center of the rock column. In the middle of the space was an upright stone. Except for the stone, the chamber was empty.

"I don't see any gold," Diego said.

"Or Solomon either," Ronnie said. "Just that stone."

Selena moved her light over the stone. A six pointed star was carved into the hard rock. In the center of the star was something that looked like a flower with eight petals. Within each point of the star was a dot.

"I think that's the seal of Solomon," Selena said

"Then we must be in the right place," Nick said.

"There's something written beneath it." Selena knelt down in front of the stone and aimed her light at it.

"Biblical Aramaic, like the scroll."

"What does it say?"

Selena pursed her lips and stared at the writing. After a few minutes she sighed.

"It's a riddle. Or a clue, take your pick."

"What do you mean?"

"I'll read it to you."

The soul of wisdom shelters with its consort in the queen's land.

"The queen's land? What the hell does that mean?"

"I don't think he's talking about Australia," Ronnie said.

"What's all that about the soul sheltering?" Diego asked.

"Soul isn't exactly the right translation," Selena said. "The ancient Hebrews believed some kind of life went on after you died, in a sort of vague limbo. The life essence of a person. There had to be something left of the body or that was the end of you. Bodies were buried and the bones preserved. Nobody cremated their dead in ancient Israel. That would've been a terrible crime."

"Doesn't sound like much of an afterlife," Diego said. "I like the idea of harps and angels better."

Ronnie said, "How do you know it's not going to be pitchforks and demons?"

Diego shrugged. "Couldn't be much worse than Afghanistan."

Nick said, "Let's think about this. Why would Ephram set this up? Leaving clues about this place in the scroll, only to tell us there's nothing here when we find it?"

"There's something else here," Selena said.

She brushed a layer of dirt and dust from the stone.

"I think it's a map."

"I can't see that it does us any good."

"That's because we don't understand it yet. That's Solomon's seal above the writing. It's a riddle you have to figure out if you want to get closer to wisdom. When Ephram writes wisdom, I think he means Solomon. So what the message says is that Solomon is with his consort in the queen's land."

"Because people associate wisdom and Solomon together?"

"Yes."

"Who was Solomon's consort?"

"He's supposed to have had over a thousand wives."

"I wonder what he was taking?" Diego said. "We knew that, we'd all get rich."

Selena ignored him. "The story of Solomon is in the Bible, in Kings. According to that version, the wives were foreigners. God told Solomon not to marry them because they would corrupt him with false gods. Solomon didn't listen. He seems to have been very attached to them. He began worshiping other gods and setting up temples for his wives to their gods. As punishment, God told him his kingdom would be scattered after his death and separated into different tribes."

"So who was his consort? If he had a thousand wives, how do we know which one the stone is talking about?"

"We have to think about it. It could be..."

Nick interrupted her. He held up his hand. "Quiet. I heard something."

They listened. "Vehicles," Ronnie said. "More than one."

"Coming up the valley," Diego said. "Now they're stopping."

"They'll be down at the foot of the slope" Nick rubbed his chin. "A four wheel drive might make it up here."

"Who'd know we're here?" Selena asked.

"Could be an Arab military patrol. Or maybe it's Al-Bayati. Get some pictures while we take a look."

Selena took out her phone and began taking pictures of the stone.

"Come on," Nick said.

They emerged from the darkness of the chamber into late afternoon light. The sun had reached the horizon and the sky was spread wide with red and vermillion streaked with black, as though the world was burning.

Nick moved with the others through the bushes to the edge of the plateau. They looked down at the valley floor. Six vehicles idled at the base of the slope. Two were pickups with heavy machine guns mounted in the back.

"That's not an Arab patrol," Ronnie said.

"They're getting ready to drive up the hill."

They went back to where Selena waited for them by the column.

"We have company," Nick said.

"Arabs?"

"There are no army markings. The Saudis don't use trucks like that. It has to be Al-Bayati."

"What do you want to do?"

"Leave. There's nothing more for us here."

The trucks began to labor up the hill in low gear.

"Too late," Diego said. "Here they come."

CHAPTER 33

Major Dov Yosef knocked on the open door of Colonel Cohen's office and went in.

"You wanted to see me?"

"The Americans are up to something. Sit down, Dov."

Dov sat. "What are they doing?"

"I just got a heads-up from Mossad. Last night they sent a stealth helicopter into Saudi Arabia from one of their carriers stationed in the Gulf of Aden. It touched down briefly in the Habala Valley near the border with Yemen, then returned to the ship."

"An insertion," Dov said.

Cohen nodded in agreement. "Can't be anything else. The question is why insert a team into that part of the country? There's nothing of any importance there."

"They must be looking for something."

"I think they're looking for Solomon's tomb and the Temple artifacts."

"How were they detected?"

"Luck. We have a Saar 4 surveillance ship observing the American carrier group. They picked it up. Otherwise we'd never have seen it."

"If there's something there, we can't let them have it. It belongs to Israel. It's our sacred heritage."

"Yes."

Cohen paused. Dov waited while his CO thought it through. "Can we put a team on site?"

"There are no units in that area. We'd have to use an airdrop and it's certain to be detected by the Saudi air defenses. Even with their technology, the Americans were lucky."

"It would be difficult on such short notice. But we can't let them escape with whatever it is they find."

"Assuming they find anything."

"There's another option," Colonel Cohen said.

"Which is?"

"Wait until the extraction, intercept their chopper and force them down where we can make sure they're not carrying something they shouldn't."

"Force down an American helicopter? What if they decide to treat us as hostile? It would go badly."

"That would be a mistake," Cohen said.

"It wouldn't do us any good to shoot them down. Besides, relations are bad enough with Washington as it is."

"Politicians never change. It's been that way since the days of the pharaohs."

"We're still in the days of the pharaohs. They just don't wear fancy headdresses or build pyramids anymore."

"No, now they build libraries named after them," Cohen said.

Dov laughed. "What are we going to do about the Americans?"

"Keep an eye on them. I've already requested that one of our satellites be tasked to observe the area."

"How soon?"

Cohen looked at his watch. "It should be coming up now."

He tapped a key. The satellite picture appeared on his computer screen.

"There it is. The light's going. We won't be able to see much in another half an hour."

The light was still good enough for the two Israeli officers to see the Americans. One of them was on top of the hill, next to one of the rock columns. Three more crouched at the edge of the slope, looking down at a half-dozen vehicles below.

"You said the Americans came in on a helicopter. What are those trucks doing there?"

"Hang on a minute."

Cohen entered a few more keystrokes. The picture appeared on a large wall monitor.

"Mechanicals. Two heavy machine guns," Dov said. "That's not a Saudi patrol. Rebels?"

"Let me zoom in."

The camera lens on the satellite bore down on the six trucks and men standing outside the vehicles. The resolution was good. One of the men looked up at the sky as if he could sense the satellite looking back at him.

Dov swore. "*Ben zona!* I know him. That's Al-Bayati. He's a puppet for Tehran, one of our problems in Lebanon."

"He must be after the same thing as the Americans."

"He's getting back in the truck," Dov said. "They're going to drive up the slope. Go back to the top of the hill."

The camera zoomed out. They watched the four Americans. Now they were all at the edge of the slope.

"They're armed," Cohen said. "Looks like MP5s or something similar."

"They're going to need more than that against those machine guns. What do you want to do?"

"Do? Nothing, except watch what happens. Maybe they'll do us a favor and take care of our Lebanese friend for us."

"You don't think we should intervene?"

"Unless you can get a unit on site in the next five minutes, I don't think we can. Even if we could, it's in Saudi Arabia. That presents a problem."

"What if they find the tomb?" Dov said.

"Then they will have saved us a lot of work. If they manage to survive whatever happens, we'll find out who they are. Once we know that, we'll apply pressure until Washington tells us what we need to know."

"President Rice won't necessarily cooperate."

"He's been friendly in the past. If he won't, somebody else will."

CHAPTER 34

One of the pickups began crawling up the hill. The others started to follow. Selena watched through her binoculars.

"They'll never make it," she said.

"What makes you so sure?"

"I've done a lot of backcountry four wheeling. There's a limit to what any of these machines will do. Those pickups will never make it up here, it's too steep and the rock is loose. The Land Rovers, maybe, if they find another route. Even so I wouldn't bet on it."

Even as she said it, the first truck churned up over some rocks and began to slip sideways in a quarter circle. Without warning it flipped over on the steep hillside. They heard the man on the gun scream as he disappeared under the truck. The wreckage began rolling down the hill, gathering speed until it smashed against an outcrop of stone at the foot of the slope. The other vehicles halted where they were. Steam rose from the wreck. No one got out.

"Amateurs," Selena said. "They should've known better."

"Gives us better odds," Diego said. "We can take these guys."

Nick took Selena's binoculars and focused on two men getting out of a Land Rover.

"Well, well. If I'm not mistaken that's Al-Bayati. And the tall guy standing next to him is the same guy that passed us when we were leaving the Museum."

"Rhoades," Selena said.

"Yeah, him. He's no amateur."

"Like we figured," Ronnie said. "They're following up on the scroll, like we are."

"I wonder if they know we're here?" Selena said.

Diego gestured down the hill. Men were getting out of the trucks.

"They're not being very careful about exposing themselves," Diego said. "I don't think they do."

"I make it a dozen, no, thirteen men, plus Rhoades and Al-Bayati. AKs."

"Figures."

"Looks like they're talking it over," Ronnie said. "How you want to handle it?"

"It'll be night soon," Nick said. "Losing that truck has got to shake them up. I don't think they'll try and come up here in the dark. We've got two choices. The first one is we slip out of here before they know we're around and call for extraction once we're out of the area."

"And the second choice?"

"We engage. Ambush them."

"Al-Bayati is the one who sent those men after Stephanie," Selena said. "We should engage."

"Do I need to point out that we're outnumbered four to one?"

"Since when has that made a difference?"

"Engage," Ronnie said.

"Let's get the bastard," Diego said.

Nick thought about it. The smart move was to leave before anyone knew they were there. Then he thought about Stephanie.

"All right," he said. "We'll take them down."

They watched as the trucks backed down the slope to the valley floor. Once they were down, Al-Bayati's men started setting up a campsite. One went over to the wrecked truck, leaned down and peered inside the cab. He straightened, looked over at Rhoades and shook his head. Two men began scavenging wood for a fire.

"They're making camp," Selena said.

"We'll let them get comfortable and watch them in shifts," Nick said. "Get some food and some sleep. We'll hit them early in the morning."

They backed away from the edge to the clear area near the column. From below, no one could see them.

"Let's see what the chef whipped up for dinner." Diego took a food ration from his pack. "Mmmm, MREs for a change. Mexican chicken stew, just like mama used to make. Makes me feel right at home."

"I've got chicken fajita," Ronnie said. "Want to trade?"

"Nah. It all tastes lousy whatever you call it."

"I had a sergeant who loved this stuff," Ronnie said. "He was always scrounging the rations people didn't want. You didn't want to get anywhere near him when his digestion kicked in."

Nick activated the comm link. In Virginia, it was morning. Elizabeth picked up.

"I was beginning to wonder. What's your status, Nick?"

"We found the tomb. There's nothing in it except a stone with an inscription and the seal of Solomon. There's a diagram on it that could be a map."

"Mm."

"We have a problem. Al-Bayati and his men showed up about an hour ago. They don't know we're here. Right now they're making camp for the night."

"One thing at a time. Tell me about the tomb and the stone."

"The tomb is in a natural cave inside one of those three columns. We were lucky we found it. The entrance was invisible. The stone is a chunk of granite inscribed with the seal of Solomon and a riddle. At least I think it's a riddle."

"What does it say?"

"The soul of wisdom shelters with its consort in the queen's land."

"What about the diagram?"

"Like I said, it could be a map. That's all I can tell you about it. There's nothing else. The seal on the rock tells us we've have found the place Ephram talked about in the scroll. There's no sign of Solomon or anything that might have been in the Temple. Just the stone."

"It must be a clue to the location of the real tomb," Elizabeth said.

"Selena thinks the word wisdom is a reference to Solomon. I think she's right. We haven't figured out the rest of it. The one thing I'm certain of is that there's nothing else here."

"You have pictures?"

"Yes."

"All right. Send them to me. Then I want you to destroy that stone."

"Destroy it?"

"It's the only way to make sure nobody else sees it."

"The only way to do that is blow it up. It could bring down that column. It looks solid but it's hollow inside and the stone is old and weathered, a little crumbly."

"Then you'd better make sure it doesn't fall on you," Elizabeth said. "What are you going to do about Al-Bayati?"

"Hit him when they're all asleep. He sent those people who shot Stephanie."

"There's no other option?"

"Not that we want to take. Especially if we destroy the tomb. I don't want him coming after us when we leave."

Nick waited while Elizabeth paused on the other end of the line. He could hear her pen tapping in the background.

"All right. Watch yourself," she said. "I'll have extraction standing by. Call when it's done."

"Copy that."

"Out."

Nick turned to the others. "You all heard that?"

Ronnie rummaged around in his pack and took out a packet of C4. The putty-like explosive could be molded against anything and was safe until detonated with an electrical charge.

"Yep. This ought to do it."

"You have timers?"

"Always."

"Getting down to that camp in the dark without making noise is going to be tricky," Diego said.

"How long do you think it will take us to get in position?"

"At least two hours. Maybe three. Steep slope, loose rocks, all that. Slower is better."

"That sounds about right. We'll give it plenty of time. Ronnie, set the charges to go off at three. When it blows, we go in."

"Do we take prisoners?" Selena.

"Not unless someone surrenders. If anyone does, be careful he doesn't change his mind."

Diego yawned. "Who's got first watch?"

"I do," Nick said. "Ronnie, go do your thing. Diego, you get some sleep. Selena, you too. I'll wake you for the next watch."

Selena moved away from the others and relieved herself in the dark, hoping there weren't more snakes in the rocks. She rearranged her uniform and went over to where Diego was already lying down with his eyes closed, his head resting on his pack. She checked the ground for anything that might bite and lay down nearby. She'd camped in the wild parts of the world many times before joining the Project. Feeling the hard ground of Saudi Arabia under her body reminded her that she wasn't twenty years old anymore and this wasn't a vacation.

She looked up at a black night sky lit with an ocean of stars. A three-quarter moon floated over the horizon in the West, casting soft, silvery light on the bleak landscape, turning it into an Escher etching of dark angles and shadows that blended into each other. It was eerily beautiful.

"A lot of stars up there," Diego said.

His voice startled her.

"Yes."

"They look different in this part of the world. I used to look up at the sky when I was a kid and think about what it would be like to fly there in a spaceship. Out where I lived was away from the city lights. I had a good view."

"Colorado, right?"

"High plains. It was flat all the way to Wyoming, which wasn't that far. When I was a teenager I'd go to Cheyenne for the big rodeo."

"Did you want to be a cowboy?" Selena asked.

"Nope. I used to watch old black-and-white Westerns with my grandpa. I wanted to be the town marshal, like Wyatt Earp. Carry a pair of six shooters and corral the bad guys. In a way, I guess I got my wish."

"What do you mean?"

"An MP5 isn't a six gun but it'll do. Seems like there are plenty of bad guys to go after. I never thought I'd find myself doing something like this."

"I know just what you mean." Selena said. "Is your family still there?"

"Yeah. It's not the same as it used to be. With the water gone, the only crop is winter wheat and that's pretty iffy. My dad gets by doing a bunch of different jobs. He's good with horses and fixing things."

"I know you're not married. Is there anyone special back there? A girlfriend?"

"There was someone a few years back," Diego said. "She decided she didn't want to be married to a soldier."

"I'm sorry."

"Nah, it wouldn't have worked out. Last I heard she got married and turned into a real nag. Joining up was the best thing I ever did."

Selena closed her eyes. The next thing she knew, Nick's touch on her shoulder brought her awake.

Ten minutes later the team started down the hill. Two and a half hours later they lay outside Al-Bayati's campsite. Snores broke the chill silence of the night. Sleeping bodies were spread in a rough circle around the dying fire, the coals a deep, red glow in the darkness. There was one tent, a lightweight model meant more for privacy than comfort. Nick guessed that Al-Bayati was inside it.

The Land Rovers and the remaining Toyota were parked nearby with men sleeping inside them. One man stood watch, sitting on a flat rock. He had an AK lying across his lap and he was nodding, half asleep. He was also on the other side of the fire. One of them would have to work around the camp and come up behind him.

Nick checked his watch. It had taken longer than he'd planned to crawl through the moonlit rocks and juniper bushes to reach the campsite. There were six minutes left before the charge went off.

He tapped Ronnie on the arm, pointed at the sentry and made a slashing motion across his throat. Ronnie nodded and crawled off, another dark shape among the dark shadows of the bushes. Nick laid his sights on the sentry, just in case. He watched the man yawn and stretch.

Ronnie rose up behind him, wrapped his hand over the sentry's mouth and pulled back his head. At the same time he drew his knife across the throat. Blood fountained out, black in the light of the fire and the moon. The man made a wet, gurgling sound. His AK clattered against the rocks.

"Hey." One of the sleeping men sat up and grabbed for his rifle. Diego shot him.

Al-Bayati's men woke and scrambled for their weapons.

Inside the tomb, the C4 went off with a sound as though someone had struck an enormous drum. A tongue of yellow flame shot from the fissure and lit the night before it died away. The narrow passage wasn't big enough to relieve the pressure of the explosion. The force of the blast had nowhere to go inside the confined space. It slammed against the hollowed out core of the pillar.

The base of the column split open, sending a burst of jagged stone hurtling into the night. Pieces rained down on the vehicles in a metallic tattoo of rock on metal. A large rock struck Diego's forearm, knocking the rifle from his hand.

The gigantic column tottered and fell in on itself like a child's tower of building blocks. Hundreds of tons of rock cascaded down the hillside. Nick wrapped his arms around his head and made himself small and prayed none of the boulders would hit him or the others. The noise was like nothing he'd ever heard, a crashing and thumping and splintering as though the end of the world had come.

Somewhere in all the noise men were screaming.

Then it was quiet.

CHAPTER 35

Al-Bayati woke when a jagged chunk of rock ripped through the top of his tent and slammed into the ground next to him. The sound of an explosion echoed from the cliffs bordering the valley. An ominous, rumbling sound urged him out of the tent. He pulled back the flap and scrambled out as an avalanche of stone rolled over the campsite. A huge boulder bounced past inches away and crushed the tent he'd just left. The air was thick with dust and screams.

The sounds of falling stone died away. Someone moaned in pain. One of his men called out to Allah, his voice strange and wet. The cry ended abruptly in a strangled cough. An automatic rifle began firing into the camp. A second joined it, then a third.

An engine started up. One of the Land Rovers careened through the destroyed campsite and pulled to a hard stop beside him. Rhoades was behind the wheel.

"Get in."

Al-Bayati scrambled in as bullets struck the car. Rhoades jammed down on the accelerator. Ahead lay what was left of the second mechanical, crushed by the rockslide. Rhoades slid around it, straightened out and headed down the valley. More rounds smashed through the rear window. Then they were out of range.

Al-Bayati looked behind him through the opening left by the shattered glass. There were only two columns standing on the hill. The third was gone.

"What happened? Who attacked us?"

"I don't know who," Rhoades said. "They blew up one of the columns and it came down on the camp."

"But why?" As soon as he said it, Al-Bayati knew the answer. "The tomb. They must have found the tomb. Or at least something like it, the place described in the scroll."

Rhoades dodged a boulder in the middle of the dry riverbed. "Makes sense."

"Get us back to the plane. I can't do anything from here."

"What are you going to do?"

"Find out who they are and what they found. If they'd found Solomon's treasure inside that column they wouldn't have destroyed it. They would have to get the gold out of there and there hasn't been enough time for that."

"Then what was there? Why blow it up?"

"To hide something. They didn't want anyone else to know what was in it. It must've been something they couldn't move."

"Then the treasure is still out there somewhere," Rhoades said.

"That's right. That means we keep looking for it."

"There aren't any more scrolls to tell us where to look."

"No. Whatever was in that column was important enough that they had to destroy it so no one else could know what it was. It could be something about the true location. We'll find out who was there. Then we'll make them tell us."

Al-Bayati's face was ugly with anger. Rhoades had seen that look before.

I wouldn't want to be one of them when he finds them, he thought.

CHAPTER 36

A flying chunk of stone gashed Selena's scalp. Blood streamed down over her face and into her eyes. She couldn't see. Next to her, Nick fired into the camp. A few of Al-Bayati's men began returning sporadic fire. She wiped her sleeve across her eyes, raised her rifle and shot at blurred shapes running through the campsite.

Ronnie's weapon began chattering. *Diego,* she thought, *where's Diego?*

A Land Rover wheeled crazily through the debris of the campsite and stopped while someone clambered in. It took off down the valley. Nick emptied his magazine after the fleeing vehicle. It kept going, leaving a billowing trail of dust in the moonlight.

The sounds of the firefight died away. Selena wiped blood away from her eyes.

"You're hit," Nick said.

"No, it was a rock. It's just a scalp wound. I'm all right."

She looked around. Diego sat on the ground, holding his right arm by the elbow. He looked like he was in pain.

Nick gestured. "Ronnie, with me."

The two men walked through what was left of the camp, looking for anyone left alive. Someone raised a rifle toward them. Ronnie shot him. The man fell back against the hard earth.

"Stupid," Ronnie said. "If Al-Bayati was still here I'm sure he'd appreciate the loyal gesture."

"He was in that Land Rover?"

"Yeah, I saw him get in. Rhoades was driving."

"Damn."

"Yeah."

There was no one left alive. They walked back to where Selena knelt next to Diego. She'd cut his sleeve away past the elbow. The forearm was bloody, the flesh ripped open.

"Que pasa, hombre?" Nick said.

"People shooting at me for years and the worst hit I've taken is from a rock. I can't believe it."

"I don't think it's broken," Selena said. "It's a nasty wound just the same. I'll bandage it up, but you need antibiotics and stitches."

"I heal quick. If it's not broken I'm not gonna worry about it."

Nick looked up at the hill. The moon was sinking. There was still enough light to see a jagged stump rising up out of the ground where the column had stood.

"You could have used a little less C4," Nick said.

"I wanted to be sure," Ronnie said.

Nick activated the encrypted satellite comm link.

"Director, you copy?"

"What's your status Nick?" Elizabeth's voice came back with an echoing delay.

"The stone is gone. So is Al-Bayati. Get us out of here."

"Is everyone all right?"

"Diego is injured. Selena got hit with debris. We're at the foot of the hill below the columns. Send the chopper here."

"What debris?"

"The column went down when we blew up the stone. She was cut by a piece of flying rock."

"The Arabs are going to love that," Elizabeth said. "Wait one."

Nick heard her talking in the background. She came back on the satellite link.

"Extraction is on the way. ETA forty minutes. Keep the link open. Out."

Selena finished wrapping Diego's arm. She stood.

"You want morphine?"

"Nah. We're not out of here yet."

Nick squatted down next to him, his MP5 cradled across his chest.

"Now you've been on a mission, what do you think? Exciting enough for you? I wouldn't want you to get bored."

"Well," Diego said, "it's not the Rangers. I guess it will do."

CHAPTER 37

Three days later everyone was back in Elizabeth's office in Virginia. Joe Eggleston sat off to the side.

"Did you have to blow up that landmark?" Elizabeth said.

"You told us to destroy the stone. It was the only way." Nick scratched his ear. "You have to admit, it did the job. No one is ever going to know what was there except us."

"The Saudis are going crazy over this."

"They don't know we were there. The only thing they're going to find are dead mercenaries who worked for Al-Bayati. The Saudis will probably think it's some kind of terrorist operation out of Yemen that went wrong."

"Let's hope you're right," Elizabeth said.

"Is Steph coming back anytime soon?" Selena asked. "She could help us find out if that diagram from the stone is a map."

"She went home yesterday. She's not going to be in for a while yet."

"It is a map," Eggleston said. "I looked at the pictures you sent and began a geographical pattern search, comparing the lines of the drawing with satellite photographs. It seemed reasonable to start in the immediate area. I got a hit right away."

Nick gave him an approving look. "Where is it?"

"The lines of the drawing form a distinctive pattern. It's a map of the Red Sea between the horn of Africa, Saudi Arabia and Yemen. Let me show you."

Eggleston tapped a key on his laptop and a satellite shot of the Red Sea and the Middle East appeared on the monitor. He zoomed in. Then he superimposed the drawing from the stone onto the photograph.

"As you can see, it's a pretty good match."

"Someone knew what they were doing when they made that," Diego said.

He was wearing a sling, mostly to keep the bandaged arm from bumping into anything. He was going to have an interesting scar. There'd been no permanent damage.

"Ephram would've been familiar with the Red Sea and the coastline," Selena said.

"Those three lines on the right could be a symbol for the three pillars," Nick said. "They're in about the right place."

"That small star of David. Where is that?" Selena wanted to know.

"Ethiopia," Eggleston said.

"And the dot near it? What do you think that is?"

"I think it's a town or settlement. The only thing in the area is a market town called Adigrat. It was there back when that stone was carved."

"What's the country like?" Ronnie asked.

"The town sits on a high plain at about six thousand feet. West from there it's all mountains and canyons."

"Sounds like a good hiding place," Nick said.

"Canyons have always been good places to hide," Ronnie said.

Selena looked at the photograph and map. "That star could mark the location of the tomb."

"What about the writing?" Elizabeth said. "About the soul of wisdom sheltering with his consort?"

Selena said, "I've been thinking about that and I still think that when Ephram says wisdom he means Solomon. If you read it literally, it says that Solomon shelters with his consort in the queen's land, meaning he's buried with her in her own country."

"But who's the consort?" Diego asked.

"I think it's the Queen of Sheba. I wasn't sure until Joe showed us this. Scholars have always argued about the Queen of Sheba, about who she was or where she came from or if she was even real. A lot of people think she ruled in Yemen. A lot of others..."

Nick interrupted her. "... think she came from Ethiopia."

"Yes. It would explain why she's called the Black Queen. In the Gospels, she's Queen of the South. That would be anywhere south of Galilee."

"I wish Lamont was here," Nick said. "His people were Ethiopian, back a ways. He even speaks the language. He could open doors for us over there."

"You think we have to go over there?"

Nick shrugged. "Is there any other option?"

Elizabeth said, "Let's not get into mission planning yet. We need a better location than a vague mark on an old drawing."

"Sure, but you know we have to pursue this. It's the only thing we've got. If Solomon's body or relics from the Temple still exist, chances are they're in those mountains."

"Going to be a bitch to find," Diego said.

"I can narrow it down some," Joe said. "If we assume the map is reasonably accurate we have enough known points of reference. There are those three marks that represent the rock columns. Then there's the dot that's probably Adigrat. Assuming the star represents the location of the tomb, I can get you in the area. After that, you're on your own."

"Work it up, Joe," Elizabeth said. "Nick, what you said about Lamont makes sense. Give him a call. See if you can get him up here for one more mission. It should be straightforward without a lot of complications. His leg shouldn't be a problem on this one."

"I'll call him when we're done."

We've never had a mission without complications, Nick thought.

CHAPTER 38

Lamont Cameron had retired to the Gulf Coast of Florida, where he'd leased a small dive shop. He'd talked about opening a shop for years before leaving the Project. Now he'd made it a reality. Nick dialed the shop number.

"Dive Paradise."

"I'm looking for a broken down, gimpy ex-Navy SEAL with an attitude. You know where I can find him?"

"Nick. What's the haps, amigo?"

"How's it going down there in retirement land?"

"The fishing's good, business sucks and the women are all too old. I'm bored out of my skull."

"I can fix that. How about a little break?"

"What kind of break?"

"Africa. Ethiopia, to be exact."

"Ethiopia? What's going on in Ethiopia?"

"Adventure. Excitement. Big doings."

"It's always big doings."

"Harker wants you back for this one. Hell, I want you back. We all do."

"Nick, you know my leg isn't as strong as it was. If we have to make a break for it on foot I'll slow us down."

"This is just an easy stroll in the mountains. Hang a closed sign on the door and get your ass up here and I'll tell you what it's about."

"Just a stroll in the mountains?"

"Yep."

"No one shooting at us?"

"Nope. No reason for anyone to know where we are."

"You want me along because I can speak the language and I look like a native?"

"Now that you mention it. Are you sure native is politically correct?"

Lamont laughed. "Why don't you ask Ronnie about that?"

"I did, once. I asked him what he thought about calling Indians Native Americans. He told me it was something some white Ivy League professor dreamed up to make himself feel better about killing all the savages. He said Indians call themselves the people or they call themselves Indians."

"Sounds about right."

"So, when can you get here? The pay's good."

Nick waited while Lamont thought it over.

"I've got a kid working for me who can keep an eye on the shop," Lamont said. "I can be there sometime tomorrow."

"We'll pick you up at the airport."

"I'll call with the flight number."

"Be good to see you."

"Yeah. You too."

Selena was standing next to Nick, listening to his end of the conversation.

"When's he coming?"

"Tomorrow."

"I'm glad. I've missed him."

"We all have. "

"You really believe what you said about nobody knowing where we're going to be?"

"How are they going to find out?"

"I don't know. All I know is that sometimes things don't work out the way we thought they would."

"It should be nice and simple," Nick said. "We go in. We find something or we don't. We leave. Nothing to it."

"Mm," Selena said.

CHAPTER 39

On the way in from the airport Nick filled Lamont in on what had happened since he'd left.

"How's Steph doing?"

"Better. Lucas says she spends a lot of time reading."

"This guy Al-Bayati sounds like a real piece of work."

"That he is."

"How's my replacement working out?"

"Diego is all right," Nick said. "He just needs a little seasoning."

Lamont smiled. "I'll bet you're just the one to do it."

Inside Project Headquarters, Diego and the others were in Elizabeth's office.

"So you're the new guy," Lamont said.

"And you must be the old guy." Diego held out his hand. "Diego Ramirez."

They shook hands. "Lamont Cameron. Nick said you were with the Rangers?"

"The 75th."

"Getting a little multicultural round here, Nick. All you need now is someone from the Air Force."

"Or the Coast Guard," Nick said.

"Are you through?" Elizabeth asked. "Because if you are, I'd like to start talking about the mission."

"Sorry, Director," Lamont said. He sat down on the couch, next to Nick and Selena.

Elizabeth sighed. "Sure you are. Sometimes I think nothing ever changes. I'm glad to see you back, Lamont."

"Thanks. I admit, I missed it."

"All right, let's get down to business. Joe has done a little snooping around with the satellite over Ethiopia. He thinks he can put you in the area where that star is marked on Ephram's map."

"Before I start, let me qualify this," Eggleston said. "I'm going on the assumption that the map is accurate and that the star is where the tomb is located. The only identifying mark in the area is the dot I think is Adigrat. Here's what I came up with using that and the columns as points of reference."

He touched a key on his laptop. A satellite photo of mountainous country appeared on the wall monitor.

"You're looking at the Tigray Region. It covers a big part of northern Ethiopia, including the city of Adigrat. It's sparsely populated. Rugged country, a lot like our Southwest with flat top mesas, high buttes and deep canyons."

The picture zoomed in until they could see the canyons weaving through the mountains. Eggleston zeroed in on one of them.

"This is west of Adigrat. There's nothing in that part of the region except a few abandoned monasteries."

"Monks lived there?" Selena asked.

"Some still do. There's a famous monastery in the area called Debre Damo. It's part way up a cliff. If you want to get in they haul you up on a leather rope."

"I'd love to see what an Ethiopian monastery is like."

"They wouldn't let you in. Men only."

"That figures."

"Anyway, this is what I've come up with."

"It still doesn't give us a specific location," Nick said. "That's a big area."

Eggleston shrugged. "It's the best I can do without more information."

"Did you try Onyx?" Elizabeth asked.

"Onyx?"

"It's a NRO system that uses ground penetrating radar."

NRO stood for National Reconnaissance Office, the Pentagon's satellite surveillance program.

"No, I didn't think of that," Joe said.

"You remember that card I showed you with the satellite and communication codes?"

"Of course. You know I have an eidetic memory."

"Onyx is number sixteen on the card. Use it to scan the target area and see if anything shows up."

"What am I looking for?"

"Some kind of underground structure. A cave or something man-made. If anything is there, Onyx will find it. The latest version is much more powerful than its predecessors."

"What if we can't pin something down with the satellite?" Nick asked.

"Then you'll have to do a ground surveillance and hope for the best. Lamont, how's your Ethiopian these days?"

"Rusty as hell, Director. My grandma made me learn. She was the only one who spoke it. I can get by but that's about it."

"Good enough. Let's see what Joe turns up with the satellites. Nick, go ahead and plan the mission based on what we know. Assume you'll be on the ground for several days. Judging from that countryside, you might have to do some climbing."

"Transport?"

"The Gulfstream will attract too much attention in that part of the world. Take a commercial flight to Addis Ababa and ship your weapons by diplomatic pouch to the embassy. Keep it light, you're not going into a war zone. Pick up everything when you get there. From Addis Ababa you'll have to go overland."

"Al-Bayati is still out there. He's been in the middle of everything and he could show up. How do you want us to handle it if he does?"

"You mean rules of engagement?"

Nick nodded.

"What do you think?"

"I think we give him an express ticket to Hell."

"Just don't let the Ethiopians catch you," Elizabeth said.

CHAPTER 40

Onyx was one of the jewels in the Pentagon's bag of tricks. The server where it lived was surrounded by elaborate firewalls and alarms designed to protect the program and alert security if someone tried to break into the system. In the brave new world of computers, satellites and universal surveillance, cyber security had become one of the first lines of defense against America's enemies.

All systems of computer security depended on elaborate compilations of sophisticated code. Like all systems, they were vulnerable to human intervention or error. The firewalls protecting Onyx were only as perfect as the programmers who had created them.

The humans responsible for monitoring Onyx were guilty of complacency. In a way, you couldn't blame them. They were convinced the firewall they'd constructed was completely impenetrable. They believed in their safeguards. In this case, it was a matter of belief creating reality, a reality that existed only in their minds.

Colonel David Cohen looked at the latest intercept of Onyx transmissions. Hacking into Onyx had been a Mossad intelligence coup. The Americans routinely shared information from the older Lacrosse GPR system. They just as routinely withheld data from the more developed Onyx platform. They were afraid hidden Iranian installations revealed by Onyx's powerful scans would become targets for Israeli retaliation.

They were right to be concerned, but it wasn't Iran that held Cohen's attention this morning. The report didn't make sense. The satellite system was targeted on an area of northern Ethiopia with no real military or strategic importance. As far as that went, most of Ethiopia fell into that category.

Why are the Americans interested in Ethiopia?

Cohen studied the scan. Onyx transmissions were routinely forwarded to his desk because of his role at the tip of the Israeli spear. They didn't look like photographs and it took specialized training to read them properly. Cohen didn't have that training. Each scan came with a report from someone who did. The technician who had analyzed this particular transmission pointed out that the uneven lines making up the recording indicated a large underground chamber with multiple levels. It was located on a remote mesa at the head of a winding canyon in the Tigray Region. The GPS coordinates were marked down. The analyst speculated that the underground structure was possibly an abandoned religious monastery. The region was dotted with forgotten retreats from the height of the Coptic monastic movement.

Very few had access to Onyx. The report identified the agency using the system. Cohen knew who they were, a secretive black ops unit that answered to the U.S. president.

The President's Official Joint Exercise for Counter Terrorism. Why is the Project involved?

Cohen had reached his command position with a combination of courage, intelligence and a gift for sensing what the enemy was thinking. He leaned back in his chair and closed his eyes and let his mind drift. Something danced on the edge of his awareness. He opened his eyes and his glance fell on the report about the American stealth helicopter that had entered Saudi Arabia.

Satellite surveillance had revealed the remains of a firefight at the foot of the hill with the three columns where Al-Bayati had been spotted. The same shot showed that one of the columns had been destroyed by a violent explosion. Cohen thought about the wreckage of two Toyotas with machine guns, and how difficult it would be to take on Al-Bayati when he had that kind of firepower. It would take a team of people highly skilled and well armed, someone like the Project or an elite special forces unit like the SEALS or his own people.

The Americans had been looking for Solomon's tomb, of that he was certain. Cohen thought about the report, the destroyed vehicles and the shattered column. He thought about the Americans using Onyx to look at Ethiopia.

They think the tomb is in Ethiopia.

The thought rippled through him as if he'd touched an electric current.

They blew up the column. There's no reason to do that unless they found something and wanted to make sure no one else would see it. Now they're looking at Ethiopia. They may have found the location of the tomb. If I were them and I thought I knew where it was, I'd go see if it was there.

Cohen picked up his phone.

CHAPTER 41

The flight to Ethiopia was uneventful. They landed at Bole International Airport in Addis Ababa early in the morning and rented a blue, four-wheel-drive Toyota Highlander, big enough for the five of them. After a stop at the embassy to pick up a trunk holding weapons and backpacks they headed north out of Ethiopia's capital on Highway 1.

Nick had decided against full combat gear and everything that went with it. He hedged his bets a little with lightweight body armor. No one except Elizabeth knew they were going to Ethiopia. There was no reason to expect serious trouble. Like Harker had said, they weren't going into a war zone.

They'd take pistols and casual civilian clothes that fit with hiking in the backcountry. Pistols were less of a problem than automatic rifles if they were stopped and easier to conceal. Not to mention that it was hard to blend in when you were wearing full combat armor.

The road was a two-lane blacktop in good condition. They settled in for the ride. Lamont drove the first shift, careful to keep to the speed limit. They stopped to eat and gas up about halfway to their destination. A roadside stand offered food and something to drink.

Diego took a deep breath. "Smells good.".

"Probably give us a good case of the trots," Nick said.

Lamont laughed. "Hey, you only live once. Ethiopian cooking is really good. My grandma used to make meals that would blow your mind."

Ragged children swarmed the vehicle as they got out. Lamont spoke to them and gave them money to watch the car while they ate.

They let Lamont order for them. The man behind the counter stared at them wide-eyed. He grinned when Lamont began talking to him. Lamont bought bottles of soda for everyone. They sat down at a rickety picnic table in the shade of a large tree while they waited for the food to be ready.

The food came. Wicker baskets with plates that had a flat piece of bread on them and a large bowl of steaming stew.

Lamont said, "The bread's a kind of sourdough called *injera.* The stew is gonna be spicy. Could be any kind of meat in it. It's called *wat.*"

He ladled out stew.

"I need a fork," Selena said.

"Nobody uses forks here. You scoop it up with the bread. Use your right hand. If you eat with the left people will be shocked."

"Why?"

"The left hand is for wiping your ass."

"What happens if you only have one hand?" Diego asked.

"Then you have a problem."

"This is pretty good," Nick said. He scooped up another bite of stew.

They reached Adigrat twelve hours after they'd left the embassy, just as the sun disappeared behind a high escarpment dotted with stunted trees. The ridge marked the beginning of the mountainous area where they were headed.

Selena watched her GPS. "I checked out hotels before we left. There's one in the center of town that should be all right. Take a right up there."

They turned off the main highway and found the hotel, a rectangular, two story building of yellow and red brick. Lamont parked and went inside while the others waited with the truck. He came out a few minutes later.

"All set. We've got four rooms. The place looks clean and they've got a café. It's a family operation, run by a father and son. The son seems like a nice guy. He told me we should hire somebody to watch the truck at night."

"I'll bet he happens to know someone," Diego said.

"That's par for the course. It's a good idea if we want wheels on the truck in the morning. He's happy to see us. We bring dollars instead of the local currency."

"What is the local currency?"

"It's called the birr. One birr is worth about four cents American."

"Let's get the trunk out," Nick said.

They went inside, showed their passports and signed the register.

"You are recommended to spray your room," the clerk said. "Very small charge." He took out four cans labeled Mobile Insecticide Spray. "Mosquitoes very bad, make you sick."

"Sick?" Selena said.

Lamont said something to the clerk in Ethiopian. The man answered him and swirled his hands in the air.

"Malaria and dengue fever," Lamont said.

Lamont paid him. They each took a can.

Selena and Nick's room had a big double bed and a balcony looking out over the city. There wasn't much to see, just blocks of low buildings stretching away across the plain. Compared to a

European or American city, there were few lights. The air smelled of dry earth and something that might have been like sage. Hints of spices and cooking oil came from the café downstairs.

"Not exactly the Hilton," Selena said, "but it's clean."

"We've stayed in worse."

There was a private bathroom with a shower stall and a small television on the dresser. Nick turned the set on. It was a news program. Children with tear streaked faces stood in the rubble of a building somewhere in the Middle East. He clicked the remote. There were only two channels. The second channel was playing an episode of Gunsmoke, dubbed in Ethiopian.

"Makes me feel right at home. Bad news on one channel and reruns on the other."

Selena said, "We'd better get something at the café before they close."

"Shall I use this stuff?" He held up the can of bug spray.

"I'd rather take my chances with the mosquitoes."

"I'm tired," Nick said. "I hope that bed is more comfortable than it looks."

"Poor baby. How tired are you?"

He arched an eyebrow at her and pretended to twirl a long mustache. "Not as tired as I plan to be later," he said.

The next morning they left the hotel just as the sun climbed above the horizon. The rental Toyota had come with two five gallon gas cans strapped in the back. Nick bought two more and gassed up. A case of bottled water went next to the gas and the trunk with their packs. Then they headed west toward the wild country.

Selena tracked their progress on her GPS.

"Turn there."

She pointed at a dirt track leading off the highway. They followed it into the wilderness until it petered out at a wide, dry riverbed exiting a deep canyon.

"This is the canyon we're looking for."

"Beautiful country," Diego said.

"Looks a lot like Arizona," Ronnie said. "Reminds me of Canyon de Chelly back home."

"Like the Grand Canyon, only not as big," Lamont said. "Or Waimea in Hawaii."

Ronnie had a closet full of Hawaiian shirts. "I've got a shirt with that on it," he said. "Nice colors."

"Is there anything that you don't have on those shirts?"

"I don't think I've got one with elephants."

"There aren't any elephants in Hawaii."

"Sure there are. In the zoo."

Lamont sighed.

Nick turned the truck up the riverbed. It wound through tall cliffs of multicolored reddish rock on either side. The going was slow, the riverbed strewn with rocks and debris that had washed down in the years when there was rain. They bumped along and Nick watched the gas gauge dropping. He thought about how much gas they had and what it would take to get back. He'd about decided it was time to stop when the decision was made for him.

They came around a turn in the canyon floor and found the way blocked by boulders. Ahead, a high mesa that marked the head of the canyon and their destination rose against a brilliant blue sky.

Nick stopped and turned off the engine.

"End of the line," he said.

"We're not moving those rocks," Lamont said.

"Nope. We'll set up base camp here." He looked at the sky. "It's already mid afternoon. We'll hike up the mesa tomorrow."

"It'll be cold later. I'll scrounge some firewood." Diego slapped at an insect. "Why does nature always come with bugs?" He looked at Ronnie. "How come they're not biting you?"

"Because I'm an Indian," Ronnie said.

"What's that got to do with it?"

"Indians and nature are friends. You don't bite your friend."

"Friends?"

"Also because I put repellent on before we left."

Diego just shook his head. Later they sat around the fire, quiet, looking into the flames. A thin column of smoke drifted into a night sky carpeted by stars. Selena broke the silence.

"I wonder if we're going to find anything," she said.

Nick got up and put more wood on the fire.

"The satellite scan says something is up there on that mesa. Whatever it is, we'll find it."

"Relics from the Temple would probably be made of gold. Even without that, the value in a religious sense is beyond price."

"It's a problem, whatever we find." Nick sat down again. "Things from the Second Temple could touch off a firestorm in the Middle East. The Israelis would see it as the final proof of their right to claim Jerusalem. As if they really needed it."

"The Arabs wouldn't like that," Ronnie said.

"Don't forget about Solomon and Sheba," Selena said. "The Israelis, the Muslims and Christians will all stake a claim."

"Sheba is important here," Lamont said. "If she's up there the Ethiopians aren't going to sit on the side and let anyone take her out of the country. Or anything else we find, for that matter."

"Great," Diego said. "We find something, everyone with a religious agenda is going to want to grab it."

"That's one way of putting it," Nick said.

"Suppose we do find Solomon and Sheba hanging out together and sitting on a pile of gold," Diego said. "What happens then?"

"I call Harker. She calls the president. It's his worry, not ours."

"Yeah," Diego said. "But he's in Washington. It's a long way from there to here."

Nick yawned. "Time to hit the rack. Who wants the first watch?"

"I'll do it," Selena said.

"Wake me in three hours."

Twenty minutes later Selena was the only one still awake. She sat on a low flat stone with her back against one of the boulders. The rock gave off faint heat from the day's sun. Moonlight filled the canyon with ghostly light. It was one of the most beautiful things she'd ever seen.

It wasn't the first time she'd found herself sitting under a foreign sky filled with stars when she was on a mission. Up to now this mission had been like a glorified camping trip. The hard metal of the pistol pressing against her hip reminded her that it could explode into sudden violence without much warning.

She thought about Solomon and the Temple he'd built to honor God, described in the Old Testament. The walls and floor had been covered with gold, she was sure. For some reason she remembered that the door had been framed in olive wood.

Solomon's Temple had been destroyed by the Babylonians in 586 BCE. It wasn't until the reign of Herod the Great that it had been rebuilt. It was said that when the Romans destroyed it for a second time, molten gold had run into the cracks of the pavement when it burned.

No one knew what had happened to the legendary treasure of the Temple. Some accounts said it had been hidden beneath the ruins, others that it had been stolen by the Romans. It had all happened a long time ago, the events shrouded in the fog of time. Now she was sitting on a rock in one of the most remote places on earth, getting ready to look for something that had disappeared two thousand years ago. You could add another thousand years if you tossed in Solomon and Sheba.

Whatever they found tomorrow, she felt the weight of that history. It was more than a fascination with archaeology and ancient artifacts. It was a sense of seeking something larger than herself, one of the great stories in the human narrative that affirmed the human connection to God.

She shivered. It felt like there was a presence nearby, something watching and waiting. It was an odd, otherworldly feeling. She looked down the moonlit canyon. Nothing was looking back.

My mind is playing tricks on me, she thought.

Just the same, the feeling stayed with her for a long time.

CHAPTER 42

They stood some distance away from the foot of the mesa. Nick scanned the massive formation with binoculars, looking for a way up. The day was clear, the sun bright in a cloudless sky. The morning was still cool before the heat of day. The mesa was hundreds of feet high, formed of reddish stone streaked with lighter colored rock.

"Looks like there's a goat track going up the side."

Nick handed the binoculars to Ronnie.

"You would need to be a goat to go up it," he said.

Selena took the binoculars and studied the narrow track as it crawled up the side of the mesa. About two thirds of the way to the top it curved around the edge of the sheer rock wall, out of sight.

"I don't think that path is natural," she said. "Look where it curves around out of sight. There are steps cut into the rock."

She handed the binoculars back to Nick. He focused on the spot.

"I think you're right."

"The tomb is up there," Selena said, "I know it is." Her voice was excited.

"Something is, anyway."

They found the beginning of the trail, crude steps cut into the side of the mesa. They were little more than depressions, rounded and treacherous, eroded by time and weather. Nick put his foot on the first one. Bits of rock crumbled away under his weight.

"Been a long time since somebody went up these," he said.

"We go slow, it should be all right," Diego said.

"Stick close to the wall. I'll lead. Diego, you take our six."

"Hey, this is a walk in the park. Nobody shooting at us."

They headed up the side of the mesa. The ground fell away beneath them. Nick was used to heights but he knew better than to look down. He kept his eyes on where he put his feet. There were places where all that remained of the steps was a short slope of crumbling rock, a trap waiting to send one of them to certain death below.

After what seemed like a long time they came to the spot they'd seen from below where the steps went around the side of the mesa. Around the curve the steps led to a wide, flat shelf shaded by a rock overhang. A dozen feet back from the edge was the outline of a cave, filled in with a wall of rock that blended in with the rest of the cliff face.

"Got to be a reason for blocking off that cave," Diego said.

"It must be the tomb," Selena said.

"Only one way to find out." Nick laid his pack on the ground. He took a long drink from his water bottle and walked over to the sealed cave. He took out his knife and began digging into the packed dirt around the rocks.

"Let's open it up."

An hour later the rocks were piled to the side, revealing an ancient wooden door.

They stood together looking at it.

Diego looked up at the overhang. "No way you'd spot this from the air."

"This might not be the tomb," Nick said. "It could be an old monastery. Either way, it's what the scan picked up."

Lamont sat down and massaged his leg.

"How's it holding up?"

"Nothing to worry about. I thought you said we were going for a stroll."

"We are," Nick said. "It's just a little more vertical than I'd figured."

"I wouldn't want to try those steps in the rain," Selena said.

"Or wind." Diego opened a bottle of water and drank.

Nick activated the comm link.

"Director, do you copy?"

A click, hissing atmospherics. Harker's voice came through after the satellite delay.

"5 x 5 Nick."

"We've reached the objective. There's a door closing off a cave in the side of the mesa. It could be a tomb or something else. We haven't gone inside yet."

"Good work."

"Once we're inside, we'll be out of contact. No way a signal is getting through this rock."

"Understood. Report back when you know what you've found."

"Will do. Out."

Nick looked at the ancient door. "Let's see if the King and Queen are receiving," he said.

CHAPTER 43

Nazar Al-Bayati was a man of many resources. One of those resources was embedded in the heart of Israeli intelligence, a man who seemed to all outward appearances a Jew. In reality he was a Shia Muslim. Jibril had been raised on the border with Lebanon and recruited by Hezbollah in his teens by a man who recognized his potential. He spoke fluent Hebrew and was a gifted liar, a survival skill he'd developed from an early age. He needed all his skills to conceal the hatred he felt for the Zionists.

His co-workers knew him as Gabriel. Not everyone who worked at Mossad was a spy. Like any large institution, most of its employees were office workers. Jibril's job was to make sure that the endless stream of paperwork churned out every day reached the right desks. In spite of email and instant file transfer there were still paper memos, assessments, reports. He was a familiar sight, wheeling his cart around Mossad Headquarters with classified material destined for one of the many offices.

Even in a world of suspicious men people like Jibril were invisible. He had become part of the daily environment, something taken for granted like electric lights or potted plants. Everyone was used to seeing him. If someone had been asked to describe him, they would've had trouble doing it.

In Mossad HQ a simple inter-office memo could contain valuable information. Everything Jibril discovered went to Al-Bayati, the man who had saved him from a life of poverty or martyrdom. The martyrdom might still come, but Jibril was untroubled by that. Death was a release and paradise waited for the faithful.

He wheeled his cart into the office of the brigadier who served as liaison with the special ops units of the IDF. Coordinated operations with military units were funneled through him for authorization. Sooner or later, they all ended up in this room. Jibril thought about the man, a self-important cog in the vast Israeli intelligence network. The general was the sort of person who thought himself above the rules that applied to others, which was why he sometimes left files unattended on his desk. It was the kind of mistake that would have gotten a lesser employee in serious trouble. As it was, there were rumors he would soon be forced to retire.

Word had reached Jibril that Al-Bayati wanted information on any operation in Western Saudi Arabia or the immediate vicinity. As he placed the day's memos on the general's desk, Jibril saw a file with the winged sword of the Duvdevan on the outer cover. He looked around. No one was watching. Jibril opened the folder. As soon as he started reading he realized this was what his patron was looking for.

Jibril took out his phone and began taking pictures of the file.

CHAPTER 44

The door into the cave was made of thick cedar, turned dark and hard by the passage of time. Iron hinges held it fast in a heavy wooden frame. A pitted ring of black iron hung in the center, mounted on a back plate in the shape of a six pointed star.

"There's the star again," Selena said.

"It opens out," Ronnie said.

Nick grasped the ring and pulled. Nothing happened.

"Figures. Give me a hand, " Nick said.

They both pulled on it. The door didn't move.

"Try twisting the ring," Selena said. "Maybe it's a lock."

Nick wrapped his hands around the ring and tried twisting it to the left.

"Nothing."

He turned it the other way. Something moved on the other side of the door and stopped.

"It moved."

He took out his KA-BAR, put the hilt through the opening and used it as an improvised lever. The ring turned with a harsh squeal of dry metal. Nick stepped back and sheathed the knife, took the ring in both hands and pulled. The heavy door scraped open.

A stale odor of faded incense and dust drifted from the opening. Selena sneezed.

They stood in the opening and Nick took out his flashlight. The halogen beam illuminated brilliant paintings in vibrant color on the walls of a large room.

"Looks like nobody's home," Nick said, "Maybe this was a monastery."

"Or a retreat."

She swung her light around and stopped on a painting. "Look at that! That's St. George slaying the dragon. Look at those colors."

They stepped inside. Diego played his light over the paintings.

"Bunch of saints, too. There's Christ and Mary."

"And the Devil," Ronnie said. He pointed. "Not somebody I'd want to run into."

The painting was a scene of Hell. Walls of flame rose around suffering black faces and bodies. The central figure was a sharp toothed, winged creature with blood red lips and open mouth, painted in vivid blue. Wide, frightening eyes stared out at the observer. The Devil looked as if he was about to step from the painting into the room. His arms were crossed around severed heads held close to his chest. A green and white snake wound around him. His legs were tied to one of his arms and he was chained to a rock. In the background, blue demons tortured agonized souls. It was a terrifying image, a grim warning of what waited for the sinner.

Every part of the room was painted. The ceiling was decorated with crosses and circles. In the middle of the ceiling was the same six pointed star that had been chiseled on the stone they'd found in Saudi Arabia.

"Must be the right place," Lamont said.

"There's another room." Diego went to it and shone his light into the space. "Looks like someone might have slept in here. There are some old coverings on the floor."

He pushed the rags aside with his foot. A cloud of dust rose into the air.

Selena sneezed. "Probably a caretaker or guardian."

Diego leaned over and picked up a large piece of paper.

"It's part of an old newspaper. It's in Ethiopian and I can't read it."

He handed the paper to Lamont.

Lamont looked at the writing. "It's an article about Mussolini and the emperor Haile Selassie, dated April 30, 1936."

"That's right before the emperor fled and Mussolini took Addis Ababa," Selena said.

"Did Mussolini's troops come this way?" Nick asked.

"They probably occupied Adigrat. Why?"

"The Italian invasion could be the reason this place was sealed off. The Coptic Church could have been worried the Italians would find what was in here."

"If that's true, why didn't anyone come back and open it up after the war was over?"

"I don't know. Maybe the people who knew about it died."

"There's another opening over here," Ronnie said.

He aimed his light into the darkness.

"Steps going down."

"You see any spiders?" Selena asked. "Webs?"

"A couple of webs, old. I don't see any spiders, though."

She turned to Nick. "Why do we always end up somewhere with spiders?"

"We haven't seen any yet. Ronnie said the webs are old. It can't be as bad as California."

"It better not be. You go first."

"What happened in California?" Diego asked.

"Long story," Nick said. "This isn't a good time to talk about it."

"There were spiders?"

"You could say that. How about you go first?"

"Why me?"

"You're the new guy, remember?"

"I don't like spiders. They had these big ugly bastards in Iraq."

"You're still the new guy. Lead on."

They started down the steps. The walls on either side of the stairway were covered with paintings. At the bottom of the steps the passage opened into a second room. There were more religious paintings, their colors bright as the day they'd been made. Aside from the paintings, the room was empty.

"That's it?" Ronnie said. "An empty room?"

"Not much to show for that climb up the side of the mesa," Lamont said.

Selena said, "These paintings are different from the ones upstairs."

Nick walked over to stand by her. "How so?"

"Well for one thing, that's Sheba over there on the back wall." She pointed at a painting of a handsome black woman dressed in vivid colors. "That fancy headdress is a crown."

Servants knelt around the figure, offering food and fruit. Sheba was looking at the next panel over. It showed a brown-skinned, white-bearded king with a look of compassion on his face, his right hand raised in blessing. His left hand held a scroll, two fingers pointing at the ground. He sat on a golden throne. A sword lay across his lap. Supplicants knelt before him.

"I think that's Solomon," Selena said.

"It could be."

"Something's not right about this."

"What do you mean?"

"Why would Ephram leave that map if this is all there is? Besides, these paintings weren't here when he was alive. They were done hundreds of years after he died. It doesn't make sense."

"Maybe there was something here back then. If there was, it's gone now," Nick said.

"There's another one of those stars over here." Lamont pointed. "It looks different."

Selena went to the wall where Lamont stood. About two thirds of the way up was the six pointed star. Like the others, it had dots within the points. Unlike the others, it had symbols around it and was chiseled out of stone instead of being painted.

"I wonder...it can't be that simple," Selena said.

Nick gave her an odd look. "Wonder about what? What can't be simple?"

"Reach up there and push against that star."

"What are you thinking?"

"Humor me. Just push it."

Nick shrugged, reached up and pushed against the stone. It moved.

There was a harsh, grinding sound and the wall with the paintings rose into the ceiling.

CHAPTER 45

Elizabeth was studying a report on Russian satellite surveillance when her secure line signaled a call.

"Yes."

"Director Harker?"

"Speaking."

"Please hold for the president."

What now?

"Good morning, Director."

Elizabeth had known President Rice for years. He sounded stressed. That was nothing new. Today she sensed an undertone of annoyance.

"Good morning, Mister President."

"I just finished a meeting with the Israeli ambassador," Rice said. "He wants to know what we're playing at in Saudi Arabia and Ethiopia. He demanded an explanation."

"Demanded, sir?"

"The Israelis know we're following up on that scroll. The ambassador reminded me that the scroll could lead to the discovery of, as he put it, 'cultural artifacts of the greatest religious significance to the Nation of Israel.' He wanted to know why we're not keeping them in the loop. He all but accused me of having found relics from the Temple and concealing them."

"What did you say to him, sir?"

"I wanted to tell him where he could put his demands and throw him out of the Oval Office. One of the frustrations of this job is that I can't do things like that without creating an international incident."

It didn't seem to require a comment. Elizabeth waited.

"Instead I told him I understood his concerns and reassured him that although we were indeed following up, nothing had yet been discovered. I also told him he would be the first to know if we found anything in Ethiopia or anywhere else."

"Did he happen to mention how he knew we were looking in Ethiopia?" Elizabeth asked.

"He did not," Rice said. "By the way, what are we doing there?"

"Based on a map we found in Saudi Arabia, I used the Onyx GPR satellite system to search for the tomb of Solomon in Ethiopia. As you know, sir, that system is highly classified. The only people who are supposed to know about Ethiopia are myself and my team. If the Israeli ambassador knew we were there, security for Onyx has been compromised."

"Wonderful. I'm sure the Pentagon will be happy to hear it."

"Yes, sir."

"What is the status of your operation, Director?"

"My team is currently on the ground in Ethiopia. They've found a location that may be the tomb. If the body of Solomon or anything from the Temple is there, they'll find it."

"When will you know?"

"They are underground and out of contact. They should be checking in soon."

"Very well. I want to know immediately if they find anything. Or if they don't."

"Yes, sir."

"Elizabeth, this is a delicate situation, as I'm sure you understand. It's imperative that anything found is kept safe. Your team has a habit of blowing things up. I don't want that to happen here."

"Yes, sir, I understand."

Rice changed the subject. "I was sorry to hear about Ms. Willits and her loss. Please convey my wishes for her quick recovery."

"I'll do that, sir."

"Keep me informed, Director."

"Yes, Mister President."

Rice ended the call.

Elizabeth considered what Rice had said. How had the Israelis discovered the team was in Ethiopia? At least this time it wasn't her responsibility. It was an issue for the Pentagon's DIA security watchdogs.

Israeli involvement complicated things. She wouldn't put it past them to send a team of their own to Ethiopia. She'd give Nick a heads-up when he was back on the surface.

Elizabeth got up and went over to the coffee set up. The pot was empty. Usually Stephanie made sure there was some on hand, ready to fuel the next hour of insanity. She was as addicted to coffee as Elizabeth, but Joe Eggleston seemed to exist on energy drinks from cans with bright colored graphics on them.

Elizabeth changed the filter, refilled it, replenished the water and turned the machine on. She waited for the coffee to brew and thought about the team. She missed Stephanie. Steph was much more than a deputy, she was a close friend. Really, the only friend Elizabeth had. Losing the baby was a terrible thing to have happen. The doctors had told her she could have another. It was poor consolation. At least she had Lucas to help her through it.

Having Lamont back was a relief, even if it turned out to be temporary. She was feeling optimistic about Sergeant Ramirez. So far he was working out just fine. It was strange to have a new face in the family, for that's what it was.

Her family.

CHAPTER 46

They walked through the doorway of the hidden room and into the past. The beams from their lights danced over a row of wooden chests piled along one wall. At the back of the room stood an altar with an elaborate Coptic cross of gold and precious stones, flanked by tall candlesticks of gold. In front of the altar were two white marble boxes, each about three feet long by two high. The walls were painted with scenes from the Old Testament. The yellow gold and jewels of the cross gleamed in their lights.

"Wow," Diego said.

"It's a shrine. Those marble chests are ossuaries." Selena shone her light across them. "There's writing on them. It should tell us who's inside."

"What are they for?" Diego asked.

"Bones."

"Like a coffin?"

"Sort of. Back then they buried the body in a temporary grave until it decomposed. Then they put the bones in chests like these. You can fit several people into one of these. It took up less space that way. No need for a sprawling cemetery using up good farmland."

"Not the kind of job I'd like. Collecting bones."

Selena knelt down by one of the chests. She traced her fingers along the writing.

Nick squatted down next to her. "What does it say?"

"This is Biblical Aramaic, an old form. It's a quotation from the Old Testament, from the Song of Solomon."

I am black but comely, O daughters of Jerusalem, as the tents of Kedar, as the curtains of Solomon.

She looked at him, eyes wide. "I think the Queen of Sheba is in here."

"How do you know where the quotation is from?"

"My uncle made sure I was familiar with the Bible. It wasn't hard, I loved the stories. It's got everything. Romance, adventure, war, sex, betrayal, you name it. Not to mention plenty of food for thought."

She turned to the other chest. Nick waited as she worked through the Aramaic in her mind.

"It's another quotation, although it's a little different from what I remember. It's from Kings."

As the Lord spoke unto David, my father, did I build a house unto his name.

"David is supposed to have been Solomon's father," she said. "This inscription is as much proof as anyone is ever likely to find that he was. That's enough to get everybody excited. According to the Old Testament, God told David that his son would build a house for Him. That would be the First Temple, the one destroyed by the Babylonians."

"Then Solomon is in there?"

"It would seem so. What's left of him, anyway."

While they were looking at the ossuaries, Diego went to one of the wooden trunks and pried loose the primitive lock holding it closed. He lifted the lid.

"Whoa," he said. "Wait till you see this."

They gathered around him. The chest was full of gold coins. Selena picked one up. She studied the face and writing stamped upon it.

"That's Herod Antipas. He ordered the death of John the Baptist and was king when Christ was crucified."

"Different from the other guy?" Diego asked.

"Yes. There were several kings named Herod back then."

"What's this?"

Ronnie had pried open another, larger trunk. It contained a structure of gold that looked like a small house with two doors. The doors were closed.

"I think that's a Torah Ark," Selena said. "There's probably a Torah scroll inside. Don't open it."

"Why not?"

"Well, because. This comes out of Judaism's holiest site. Only a Rabbi is supposed to open it and we should honor that. If that holds the Torah scroll from the Temple, the Israelis are going to be ecstatic when they get this back."

"If they get it back," Nick said.

"Why wouldn't they?"

"It's as much political as it is religious. Rice might decide to use it in the big game. It's a powerful bargaining chip."

"You think he'd keep it from the Israelis?"

"I don't know. That's not my call. When politics gets involved what's right tends to go out the window. Even Rice has to answer to people who don't always make good decisions."

"Are we going to take any of this with us?" Lamont asked.

"I don't think so. That ark is made of solid gold and heavy. I don't see us carrying it or any of these chests down those steps even if we wanted to. It's amazing someone managed to get all this gold up here."

"What do you want to do with it?"

"Leave it right where it is, along with everything else. We found what we were looking for. Now we go home and let somebody else worry about it."

"I know you're right but I don't like it," Selena said. She gestured at the ossuaries. "We should make sure there are actually bones inside before we go."

"Good idea. Give me a hand, guys."

They lifted the heavy lid covering Solomon's ossuary and rested it against the wall. Inside were the bones of a single skeleton. The empty eye sockets of the skull seemed to look at them. A small, wooden box made of cedar lay next to the bones. Nick reached down and lifted it out. He opened the box. Inside was a large gold ring with a raised design of the six pointed star with writing around it. He took it out and shone his light on it.

Selena drew in a breath. "My God. I think you just found the seal of Solomon. I always thought it was a myth."

"What does the writing say?" Nick held his light on the ring. "Weird. It feels warm to the touch."

"I don't know what it says. It's in a language I've never seen before."

"I don't think I've ever heard you say that. What's the big deal about this anyway? Every king has lots of jewelry."

"Not like this," she said. "This ring is supposed to have magical powers, given to Solomon by God."

"What kind of powers?"

"The power to control the wind was one of them. He's supposed to have been able to call upon the wind if he needed to defeat his enemies. It would be a handy thing in the desert against an invading army. You could bury them in a sandstorm. He could talk with animals. The ring also gave him the power to control the jinn."

"Okay," Diego said. "Who are the jinn?"

"Not who, what. They're beings who live in a different dimension and interact with humans."

"Like angels?"

"No, the jinn are different. In Islam there are a lot of stories about them. Remember Aladdin and his magical lamp?"

"With the genie?" Ronnie said.

"Genie and jinn are the same thing. Solomon was supposed to have enslaved them with the ring. There's a story in Islam about Solomon's death. He dies leaning against his staff, which keeps him propped up. All the jinn think he's still alive so they keep doing the things he told them to do. Then God sends a worm to gnaw through the staff until Solomon falls down. That's when the jinn realize they're free. As I recall, they were a little pissed off about it."

"I guess they weren't very smart," Lamont said.

"I suppose not," Selena said. "Can I see that?"

She took the ring from Nick. "This is like finding King Arthur's sword, except it's real and not just a story."

"Maybe it's not the seal," Nick said.

"What else could it be? There's no reason to put it with Solomon's bones if it isn't."

"Maybe we should try calling up a genie," Lamont said. "One who's good-looking, like in that old TV show."

"It's not something to joke about," Selena said. "A lot of times there's something real behind a legend."

"Come on," Diego said. "You don't believe in genies, do you?"

"Maybe not in genies," Selena said. "There are physicists who will tell you there are other dimensions existing right along with ours. There might be beings who live in them. There could be some part of the legend with a basis in reality."

"You been smoking something, Selena?" Lamont asked.

Selena ignored him and handed the ring to Nick. She took out her phone and began taking pictures of the writing on the ossuaries.

"I'm going to keep the ring as physical proof, Nick said. "We've seen enough. Time to let Harker know what we've found."

He climbed back up to the top level and into the front room. After the darkness of the tomb, the light outside was blinding.

Nick stepped into the bright sun. He squinted and held the ring up to look at it.

"I'll take that," a voice said.

CHAPTER 47

Al-Bayati and a half dozen men carrying AK-47s were positioned on either side of the entrance. A seventh man held a grenade. He looked as though he should be playing in the ugly man basketball league. He was almost seven feet tall, with a jaw like a crocodile and crooked eyes. Standing next to him was a man Nick recognized as the former MI6 agent, Addison Rhoades. Rhoades smiled.

Al-Bayati reached out and took the ring from Nick's hand. Rhoades took his pistol.

"Raise your hands. Call the others out."

"Al-Bayati," Nick said in a loud voice. He raised his hands. "You're a surprise. What others?"

"Please, show some respect. I know who you are and I know the rest of your team is with you. Tell them to come out with their hands up," Al-Bayati said, "or Badr will toss that grenade into the cave. Your friends wouldn't like that."

He gestured at the ugly man. Badr grinned at Nick, showing a mouthful of rotten teeth. The others heard Nick say Al-Bayati's name and the threat as they entered the front room.

"There's a room farther in, down a flight of steps on a lower level," Nick said, keeping his voice loud. "That's where I got the ring. The others are down there, looking through the rest of what we found."

"What did you find? Solomon? Gold?"

"Well," Nick began," yes, Solomon's down there. So is Sheba. There are wooden trunks. Lots of gold coins..."

Nick kept talking, stalling for time. Inside the tomb, the others huddled where they couldn't be seen from the entrance.

"We've only got one shot," Ronnie said. His voice was barely a whisper. "They can't see us back here in the dark. We stick to the walls until we get to the sides of the doorway. Then we come out shooting."

"What about Nick?" Selena asked.

"It's what he'd do," Lamont said. "Al-Bayati can't let us go. We give ourselves up, we're dead. Nick knows that. He knows we have to try."

"He's right," Diego said.

Selena nodded. They split and moved to the front and took up positions on either side of the door.

"Enough." Al-Bayati cut off Nick's running monologue on the treasure of the Temple. "Call for your friends, or the grenade goes in."

"You do that, you'll bring down the rock and seal it all up."

"It's a chance I'm willing to take," Al-Bayati said. "I have what I came for."

He placed the ring on his finger.

"Tell me something," Nick said. "Are you the one who sent people after us in Virginia?"

"That was my operation," Rhoades said. "Too bad it didn't work out or you wouldn't be in this nasty situation, would you? You should have left it alone, Carter."

Nick's ear began itching and burning.

Showtime, he thought. His heart began pounding as adrenaline rushed through his body.

Al-Bayati's Skorpion pointed at Nick's gut. The muzzle was too close, the kind of mistake an amateur might make, or someone who was overconfident. Nick knocked the gun sideways in a hard, sweeping motion and shouted at the same time. Al-Bayati's finger was on the trigger and the gun fired, sending a three round burst into one of his henchmen. Nick drove his elbow into the side of Al-Bayati's head. Pain exploded in his arm.

Selena, Ronnie, Diego and Lamont burst from the doorway firing their pistols. Al-Bayati's men weren't wearing armor. Three went down with the first shots. Al-Bayati lay where Nick had knocked him to the ground. Selena's gun jammed as she fired at the ugly man. Badr snarled at her, stepped forward and slammed a huge fist into her face. She went down as if she'd been hit with a hammer.

The ledge was chaos. Everyone seemed to be shooting at once. Selena was on the ground, Al-Bayati on his knees. A round seared Nick's leg, hot and burning. He saw Rhoades aiming at him.

"Bye," Rhoades said.

There was a shot. Rhoades got an odd expression on his face. He looked down at a red blotch spreading across the front of his shirt. He stumbled backward, trying to raise his rifle. There were two more shots. Rhoades staggered and took another step back.

It was a step too far. He went over the edge and disappeared. His scream lasted for what seemed like a long time before it suddenly cut off.

Nick turned back and froze. Badr held Selena upright. Blood streamed from her nose and down over her shirt. She looked dazed. Al-Bayati hid behind Badr with his gun pressed against her head.

"Stop or I kill her," he shouted.

Ronnie and Lamont stood in the doorway of the tomb with their pistols pointed at Al-Bayati. Diego lay on the ground between them in a widening pool of blood. He wasn't moving.

"Ronnie, hold it," Nick called.

"Put the guns down," Al-Bayati ordered.

"I don't think so," Nick said. "Looks to me like a standoff. You shoot her, you're a dead man and your buddy too."

"I'll do it."

Nick shrugged. "Go ahead. You're not leaving here if you do."

Al-Bayati looked at Lamont and Ronnie, their pistols pointed at him. Their faces were grim. He licked his lips.

"I'll make you a deal," Nick said. "You let her go, we let you go. You've got the ring. It's what you wanted, right? She's hurt and I have a man down. They're my priority, not you."

"You really think I'd trust you?"

"I don't see as you have much of a choice," Nick said. "You kill her, we kill you. Simple. She's in no shape to go down those steps. I can't leave her and Diego here like that and come after you. Take the ring and leave and let me take care of my wounded. You'll be long gone by the time I do that."

"I'll take her with me."

"She'll slow you down," Nick said. "And if she should slip and fall off, I won't rest until you're dead. I promise you that. You know who I am, don't you?"

"Yes." Al-Bayati spat the word out. "I know who you are, Carter."

"Then you know I mean what I say. I promise that if you let her go, I won't follow you down the steps."

"He lies," Badr said.

"Shut up."

"That's right, ugly, shut up. Your boss knows it's your best chance at getting out of here alive."

Selena sagged in Badr's hold. Blood trickled from her nose.

"All right, Carter. Let her go, Badr."

Badr looked unhappy but did as he was told. Selena fell in a heap onto the rock floor of the ledge and lay there. She stirred and groaned.

"I can still shoot her," Al-Bayati said.

He began to back away toward where the steps started down. Badr followed, keeping his gun pointed at the others.

"If anyone tries to follow us you will be, how do they say, sitting like turkeys."

"Ducks," Nick said, "like sitting ducks. Not turkeys."

"Yes, like ducks. Dead ducks. Easy to shoot." He held up the ring. "This will protect us."

"Good luck with that," Ronnie said.

"Can it, Ronnie." Nick said.

Al-Bayati still had his gun pointed at Selena. "Come, Badr."

The two men reached the steps, started down and disappeared around the corner.

"Selena." Nick went to her.

She was conscious, her eyes open.

"Selena, talk to me."

"What?"

Her eyes focused on him. "Nick?"

"You got punched. Your nose is broken."

"The others?"

"Al-Bayati's gone. Diego's hurt. I don't know how bad yet."

He looked over at Ronnie and Lamont. Ronnie was pressing a bandage on Diego's chest. Pressing hard.

Shit.

"You all right now?" Nick asked Selena.

"I think so. Dizzy."

Nick helped her stand and walked her over to the others, away from the edge of the cliff and the long drop to the bottom.

"Sit here."

Ronnie knelt next to Diego. He'd stopped pressing on the bandage. His hands were covered with blood. He looked up at Nick.

"Diego?" Nick asked.

Ronnie shook his head.

"He took two rounds, one low, one in his chest. They went right through that light armor like it wasn't there. He's gone."

"Fuck," Nick said.

"Yeah."

"All right. We'll give Al-Bayati time to get off the steps and then we'll carry him down."

"You're really going to let him leave?"

"We know where he lives. He's a dead man walking, he just doesn't know it yet. There's no cover going down, it's too exposed. He can pick us off."

Nick looked down at Diego's body. *What a waste*, he thought, *and for what?*

Lamont was working on Selena.

"This will hurt," he said. "Your nose is broken. I'm going to put it back in place and tape it. Okay?"

"I'm going to kill that ugly bastard next time I see him. Yow!"

Lamont pushed the cartilage back in place with a sudden movement of his thumbs while she was talking. He taped it in place.

Tears of pain ran from her eyes. "You could've warned me," she said.

"I told you it would hurt. You're going to have a couple of real shiners in an hour or two," he said.

"Diego's dead?"

"Yeah."

"He kept saying he was glad nobody was shooting at us."

"One of the reasons I quit before," Lamont said. "It's better when no one's shooting at you."

"We missed you," Selena said.

"I'm back now. Anyway we have to catch up with Bayati. That might take a while. I guess I'll stick around."

The adrenaline rush from the fight was gone. Nick felt like he was eighty years old.

Nick activated the satellite link.

"Director, you copy?"

"Nick, what's your status? My visuals are down."

Harker's voice was clear.

"Everything turned to shit. We found the tomb. Then Al-Bayati showed up. Diego is dead."

"What? He's dead?"

"Affirmative."

"What about Bayati?"

"He's gone. I had to let him go or he would've killed Selena. All of his men except one are dead. Bayati's pet spy is dead."

"Rhoades?"

"Yes. He sent those people after us in Virginia. Tell Lucas."

There was silence over the link. Nick waited.

"What's in the tomb?"

"Solomon, the Queen of Sheba, and a lot of gold and artifacts from the Second Temple. It looks like it was a Coptic shrine. There's a big jeweled cross on an altar. We even found the Seal of Solomon. Al-Bayati has it. Director, we need extraction."

"Where are you now?"

"On the ledge in front of the tomb. We'll start down soon with Diego. I'm not leaving him here."

"We have a carrier group in the Aden Sea. I'll arrange a chopper to pick you up." She paused. "I'm sorry about Diego."

"Yeah. Out."

"How long are we going to give that scumbag?" Ronnie asked.

"An hour ought to do it. I want to make sure he's gone. He was right about us being sitting ducks on those stairs. It's not worth the risk. Like I said before, we know where he lives. We'll catch up with him later."

An hour later they were getting ready to start down when Lamont said, "There's a bird coming right toward us."

"That's a Black Hawk," Ronnie said.

Nick activated the link.

"Yes, Nick."

"Director, there's a chopper headed our way. Military."

"It's not one of ours," Elizabeth said. "Extraction for you is about to leave."

Ronnie had his binoculars focused on the approaching aircraft.

"Israeli markings."

"Director, the bird is Israeli. It will take us a couple of hours to get down," Nick said. "All they have to do is wait for us."

"It will take a couple of hours to get someone to you," she said. "Keep the link open."

"Copy."

"I'm going to call the White House. It's time to get the Ethiopians involved. Try not to create an international incident."

"It might be a little too late for that," Nick said.

CHAPTER 48

Dov Yosef watched the Ethiopian countryside slip past underneath his helicopter. He was riding in a Sikorsky UH-60 Black Hawk, one of the new versions purchased from the Americans. *One thing you can say about the Americans,* Dov thought, *they make good helicopters.* This one had been launched from the INS Eilat, one of three Saar Class Corvettes in the Israeli Navy, the same ship that had spotted the stealth helicopter sneaking into Saudi Arabia. The chain of events that started then had led to Dov and his men flying over this remote wilderness.

It was amazing how quickly politicians could get something done if it really needed to happen. The potential for recovering artifacts from the Second Temple had lit a fire in Jerusalem. Dov's helicopter was supposed to be part of an official Israeli mission to explore the possibility of upgrading the Ethiopian military with the Iron Dome air defense system developed by the Israelis. He would be tracked by the outdated SAM sites deployed by the Ethiopian Air Force but not fired upon.

The radio intercom in his helmet crackled.

"Major, we have the objective in sight. Sir, there are four people on a ledge high up on the side of a mesa. Looks like a cave behind them."

"What's the access?"

"A trail going up. They've spotted us. One of them has lenses on us."

"Hostile?"

"Can't tell, sir. There are bodies on the ledge. It looks like there was a fight and casualties."

"Find the trailhead and land as close as you can. We'll wait for whoever it is to come down."

"Yes, sir."

The engine note changed as the chopper banked sharply to the left and the pilot began his descent. They set down on a flat area not far from where the steps began to climb up the side of the bluff.

Dov deployed his men between the helicopter and the trailhead. He studied the bluff through binoculars and adjusted the focus. From where he stood he couldn't see the ledge and the cave. Only the trail of primitive steps.

Dov let the binoculars hang by their strap and took out a green pack of Noblesse cigarettes. He shook one out and lit it. He'd been warned more than once to quit. It didn't matter, there was nothing like a smoke when he needed to think.

Like now.

There were bodies on the ledge. Something in the cave had to be worth fighting over. If it was the body of Solomon or treasure from the Temple he was sitting on top of political and religious dynamite.

Dov took another drag, stubbed out the cigarette and put it back inside the pack. He raised the binoculars again and watched as a man wearing civilian clothes and armed with a pistol on his hip came into view and started down the steps. He was followed by a woman dressed like a hiker. Adhesive tape was plastered across her nose and there was blood on her shirt. She wore a holstered pistol and was followed by two men carrying a third between them. They were having a hard time on the narrow, crumbling steps, moving at a snail's pace. Dov looked at his watch. He estimated they would reach him before sundown.

Two and a half hours later the team reached the bottom. Nick and Ronnie gently set Diego's body down on the dry earth. Nick looked at the Israeli major and the hard looking men who were pointing Tavor assault rifles at them.

"Special ops," Nick said to Ronnie.

Dov stepped forward. "I'm Major Yosef. Please keep your hands away from your weapons. You are American?"

"That's right."

Dov looked at him. "I know you. You were in Jerusalem, when they tried to kill your president."

Nick nodded and rubbed his arms, sore from carrying Diego down the side of the bluff.

"Nick Carter. I wish you had gotten here sooner, Major."

"You've lost a comrade. I'm sorry, Mister Carter, but tell me why are you here."

"I think you know why we're here."

"The scroll led you to this place?"

"Two scrolls. Yes, they led us here. And if you're wondering whether or not Solomon is up there, he is. So is the Queen of Sheba."

"You're joking."

"No. She really is up there."

Dov signaled his men to relax. He took out his cigarettes.

"Smoke?" He took one out and lit it.

"No thanks," Nick said.

"What else is in the tomb?"

"Gold, a lot of it. Relics from the Second Temple."

"Ah."

"I'm sure your government will be happy to hear that."

"What happened?" Dov gestured at Diego's body.

"There's a Lebanese scumbag named Al-Bayati."

"I know who he is."

"He showed up with a half-dozen men. That's what happened."

"Is he up there?"

"No, he's gone. He must have made it out just before you got here. He took something of Solomon's with him. A gold ring with symbols on it."

"It was Solomon's seal," Selena said. "I'm sure of it."

Dov turned to her. "How do you know this?"

"I've studied the period and I know the stories. The ring was the one thing Al-Bayati wanted above everything else. I always thought the seal was a myth. It's clear Al-Bayati believes the ring has real power. He said it would protect him. It was in an ossuary with Solomon's bones, the only other thing in there. What else could it be?"

"You should listen to her, Major. She knows what she's talking about."

The voice of the pilot came through Dov's headpiece. "Sir, there's a helicopter approaching."

"Identity?"

"American, sir."

Nick heard rotors coming closer. He looked up and saw a gray CH-53 Sea Stallion with Navy markings heading for them.

"Here comes the cavalry," Nick said.

"Maybe you could use another word to describe our rescuers," Ronnie said.

"You getting sensitive in your old age?"

"My people have not had good experiences with the cavalry."

"You called them here?" Dov asked Nick.

"My boss did."

Dove started to say something when the pilot's voice sounded again in his ear. "Sir, there's a call for you."

"Patch it through."

"Major Yosef."

Dov recognized the voice of Colonel Cohen. "Colonel."

"The U.S. president has been talking to the Israelis You have found the tomb of Solomon?"

"Apparently, sir. I've not yet had a chance to verify the contents. There are Americans here who say it is. They also say that gold and artifacts from the Temple are inside."

"That is what their president told our prime minister. You are ordered to secure that tomb and prevent any further intrusion."

"Understood. Colonel, an American helicopter is about to land."

"You have your orders, Dov. No further intrusion. That includes the Americans. You are authorized to use all means necessary."

Dov looked at Nick and the others. "The Americans told me something was stolen from the tomb by Al-Bayati."

"What was taken?"

"They say it was the Seal of Solomon."

Cohen swore. "That pig. He defiles everything he touches."

The Navy helicopter touched down and a squad of Marines piled out in full battle gear. Yosef's men had already taken up position to protect their aircraft.

"Better caution your men," Nick said. "We don't want any mistakes."

"My orders are to secure the site," Dov said.

"Of course they are. And now you have help."

A Marine lieutenant commanding the squad made his way across the distance between the two choppers and stopped. He was about six feet tall, tanned and fit. His camouflage battle dress was clean and crisp, his polished boots just beginning to show dust from walking over to them. Dov had no rank insignia on his uniform. That was standard for his outfit in the field.

"Who's in charge?" The lieutenant said.

"I am." Nick and Dov spoke at the same time.

The lieutenant looked at the two of them. "Are you Major Carter?" He addressed Nick by his old rank.

"Yes."

"Lieutenant Axton, sir." He saluted. "I've been instructed to inform you that elements of the Ethiopian military are on the way here. My orders are to take you back to my ship."

"Wait just a second, Lieutenant."

Axton looked at the Israeli major. "Who are you? Sir."

Nick interrupted. "This is Major Yosef. He's been ordered by his government to secure this area."

"Those are my instructions as well. I'm to post some of my people here before I leave."

"The contents of that tomb are the legal and historical property of Israel," Dov said.

"The Ethiopians may have something to say about that," Nick said.

The Israeli's face was tight. "The only people guarding it will be mine."

"Sorry, sir. I have my orders and I will carry them out."

Nick almost smiled. Axton reminded him of himself when he was younger.

"I don't think you want to take on my men," Yosef said.

"I don't think you want to take on mine," Axton said.

Nick interrupted. "There's no need for a pissing contest. Nobody's going to take anything out of that tomb until the big shots figure out how to handle it. Major Yosef, you're forgetting something."

"What's that?"

"We're on Ethiopian soil and this is a sacred site for them. The tomb is a shrine of the Coptic Church, as you'll see for yourself. Addis Ababa is sure to make a claim on everything in it."

Selena had been watching the testosterone levels building.

"If I could make a suggestion?"

Nick and Dov turned toward her. Lieutenant Axton gave her an appreciative once over.

"Nick's right. Nothing is going to happen here until the politicians sort it out. Major, there's no reason why Lieutenant Axton's men and yours can't post a joint guard. I assume that would be all right with you, Lieutenant?"

"Yes ma'am, I think it would. As long as my men are on site to prevent any unauthorized access. Nothing is to be removed. By the Israelis, the Ethiopians or anyone else."

"Major?"

"It's a solution," Yosef said. "No one except my men are to go inside the tomb. The objects in there are sacred to us."

Axton said. "We don't have to go in as long as nobody takes anything out."

This young officer will go far, Nick thought.

"Agreed," Yosef said.

"Thank you sir. With your permission, I'll have my Sergeant pick men to work with you. Perhaps you would like to do the same?"

"Very well."

"Then I'll get to it." Axton saluted and turned to Nick. "When you're ready, sir."

"Thank you, Lieutenant."

Dov watched Axton go back to his men. "Not much seems to bother him."

"He's a Marine," Nick said. "What else would you expect?"

"More company coming," Lamont said. "Looks like the Ethiopians are joining the party."

He pointed off to the east. Two military helicopters were headed their way.

"Let's get out of here," Nick said. "I've seen enough of Ethiopia for a lifetime."

They picked up Diego's body and headed over to the American helicopter.

*****

Al-Bayati and Badr had reached their vehicles an hour before the Israeli helicopter landed. They'd stopped at the same spot where Nick had left the Toyota.

"Disable all of them except one," Bayati said. "Tear out the wires."

It only took a few minutes. Al-Bayati and Badr got in the last vehicle and drove away.

Badr drove. Al-Bayati felt the glow of Solomon's ring in his hand and thought about what he would do when he got back to Lebanon. He'd bind the ring to him with the blood sacrifice, as the ancient book of magic passed down to him by his ancestors instructed.

The book dated from before the thirteenth century, a collection of Arabic incantations and formulas copied with painstaking care onto pages of yellowed vellum. Among its secrets was the hallucinogenic formula of the *Hashishin,* Hassan-i-Sabbah's society of assassins. Sabbah had used it to reveal paradise to his followers and control them. Al-Bayati used it for pleasure. It was the drug Rhoades had preferred.

Thinking of Rhoades soured Al-Bayati's mood. He'd been a useful asset and it would be difficult to replace him. Badr could be trained to perform the part Rhoades had played in the monthly ritual, it was simple enough and Badr could be trusted. Someone else would have to be found to take the dead spy's role in the West.

Al-Bayati felt cheated. To have come all this way and then to have been denied entrance to the tomb. Denied the gold, the pleasure of holding Solomon's skull in his hands, because of meddling Americans. It was unfair. He imagined exploring Carter's capacity for pain with one of the ancient instruments of torture he had in his collection. As for the woman, his thoughts turned to how acceptable she would be as an offering to the god, after he'd sampled her wares, of course. The god didn't care about that. It was unlikely he would see either one of them again. If he ever had the opportunity, Al-Bayati vowed he would turn imagination into reality.

CHAPTER 49

Nick looked out the window of the hotel room in Addis Ababa at a row of flags flying in front of the United Nations conference center. He was waiting for new instructions from Elizabeth. Diego's body was waiting for shipment back to the states, courtesy of the U.S. Navy.

Selena came out of the bathroom wrapped in a hotel robe, combing her hair.

"It's good to get clean again," she said.

"Yeah."

She walked up behind him and put her arms around him and leaned against his back.

"I liked him," she said. "It was too quick. I hardly knew him."

"It's better quick than slow. It still stinks. You know what bothers me?"

"What?"

"I keep thinking that if someone had to get it, I'm glad it wasn't you or Lamont or Ronnie."

"And you feel guilty about that? About caring more for your friends than for someone you've only known for a little while?"

Nick was silent.

"I understand but I'm not sure that's what's bothering you."

"What do you mean?"

"I think what bothers you is that you couldn't stop what happened. It could have been any one of us. You knew we'd have to come out of that room shooting."

"If you hadn't, Bayati would have killed all of us."

"That's right. And you couldn't have known he'd show up," Selena said.

"I should have been prepared. I should've anticipated it."

"How? There wasn't any reason to think he knew about Ethiopia. We blew up the stone with the map. This wasn't supposed to be a combat mission, it was supposed to be a reconnaissance."

"Yeah, but recon has a funny way of changing into something more lethal."

"In a war zone, that makes sense. In this case it doesn't make any sense at all. It's not your fault Diego is dead."

Nick turned away from the window. "I know you're right. It's not the first time I've lost someone. I've never gotten used to it."

"That's why you're one of the good guys," Selena said.

Nick's satellite phone signaled.

"It's Harker." He made the connection. "Yes, Director."

"I spoke with the president. You're leaving for Turkey."

"What's in Turkey?"

Selena heard his end of the conversation. She raised her eyebrows in surprise.

"Incirlik Air Base. Transport will be in Addis Ababa tomorrow. A driver from the embassy will pick you up at your hotel and take the four of you to the airport. Keep your guns. You're getting on an Air Force plane. At Incirlik you can fit yourself out with the gear you need."

"Where are we going after that?"

"President Rice has been talking with the Israeli prime minister about what you found. By the way, you are all up for an Israeli Medal of

Distinguished Service. It's quite an honor for a foreigner."

"It won't do Diego much good," Nick said.

"No, it won't. What I'm about to tell you might make you feel better."

"Go on."

"Rice and the Israeli PM agree that Al-Bayati must not be allowed to keep possession of Solomon's Seal. Various options were discussed, most of which resulted in an assault on his compound that would likely start a new war. The Israelis would like to go storming in there but they have their hands full with the Shia/Sunni civil war heating up. The president and the prime minister feel a military assault is not expedient."

"Where have I heard that before?" Nick said. "Usually when politicians say something isn't expedient they're ducking responsibility or they have something up their sleeve."

"This time it's you they have up their sleeve," Elizabeth said. "Al-Bayati is back in his villa. From Turkey you're going to Lebanon. Your instructions are to get into that compound, find that ring and get out again. While you're there, nobody would be upset if you took out Al-Bayati."

"How am I supposed to do that? That place is damn near invulnerable."

"I'm sure you'll figure something out," Elizabeth said.

CHAPTER 50

Incirlik AFB was in the south of Turkey near
the city of Adana, not far from the Mediterranean
and the coast of Syria and Lebanon. They were met
at the plane and taken to guest quarters reserved for
visiting VIPs like the Secretary of State.

Lamont looked around the suite of rooms that
had been assigned to them.

"Nice digs," he said. "My mom would've liked
that chandelier."

"Your tax dollars at work," Nick said. "The
president must've told them to give us the royal
treatment."

"Why is it that the big shots always seem to
need stuff like this?" Ronnie said.

"It makes them feel important."

"It makes me feel like I'm on a movie set,"
Lamont said. "Seems like there might be better
ways to spend the money. Like better armor for our
guys. Stuff like that."

"Tell that to Congress," Selena said.

"I already have, along with a lot of other
people. Problem is they never listen."

"Better enjoy it while you can," Nick said.
"We're leaving as soon as we figure out how we're
going to do this. Harker sent satellite shots of the
compound. She's waiting for us to tell her what we
need."

He pressed buttons on his phone. "The photos
are supposed to show up on that monitor over there
on the desk. I can't get it to work."

"Give it to me," Selena said.

She did something with the phone and the pictures of Al-Bayati's compound appeared on the screen.

"How did you do that?"

"I'll show you another time," she said.

Ronnie studied the shots. "When were these taken?"

"This morning," Nick said. "Why?"

"It's different than the last time we looked." Ronnie pointed at the gate and the street outside. "His security is Hezbolla, right?"

"That's right."

"So where are they?"

The four of them contemplated the photos. There were civilians passing by the compound but the armed thugs they'd seen before were gone.

"Still looks like trouble," Lamont said. "He's got men inside the walls and they've moved that Quad .50 into the center of the courtyard, covering the gate."

"Not as many men," Nick said.

"Something must have pulled them off," Ronnie said. "Is there another war starting up?"

"A lot of them are going to Syria to fight the Sunni rebels," Selena said. "That might have something to do with it."

"Whatever the reason, it's good news for us," Nick said.

"I don't think we can climb up on the water side," Lamont said. He pointed at a swirling chaos of water and foam where the Mediterranean broke against the cliff. "Those rocks at the base would cut a zodiac to pieces and there are whirlpools. The currents would suck us under before we got close enough."

"Then it's the walls or the gate."

"I don't like the walls." Ronnie pointed at the razor wire. "Aside from the wire, they're high and everything is lit up at night. We'd be spotted and picked off."

"That gate looks like something from a crusader castle," Lamont said. "All that's missing is a moat. If they don't want to open up we're not getting through it without blowing it."

"That will attract too much attention. We can't do that."

"There are no windows on the ground floor. Al-Bayati is a little paranoid, isn't he?" Selena said.

Ronnie nodded. "He should be. He's got good reasons."

"Now he's got four more," Lamont said.

"If we don't go up the cliff in back and we don't go over the wall or through the gate, I guess we'll have to drop in on him," Nick said.

"You want to use a chopper?"

"You have a better idea?"

"What about that Quad .50? If they don't like what they see, they'll blow us right out of the air with that baby."

"We don't have to use a helicopter," Selena said. "We can make them open the gate."

Nick looked at her. "How do you plan to do that?"

"Al-Bayati has a big ego, right? What if we think of something that strokes his ego? Something that makes him want to open the gate for us?"

"Like?"

"Like a television interview, say from Al Jazeera. We set it up ahead of time."

"What's the hook?"

"Doesn't he contribute to the cause? Hospitals for the fighters, things like that?"

"Shia fighters. Al Jazeera is biased towards the Sunni."

"They make a token effort to appear balanced and the Shia/Sunni thing is big news right now. If Al-Bayati thinks they're going to present a program showing him in a favorable light he might go for it."

"Let me guess," Ronnie said. "You're supposed to be the interviewer."

"Why not? We steal one of Al Jazeera's vans and pull up to the gate. His guards see me step out of it dressed like a Muslim woman should be, someone who's expected. They'll relax. They open the gate, we drive into the compound and that's when we take them out."

"It could work," Lamont said.

"You have a devious mind," Ronnie said to Selena.

"You just figure that out?" Nick said.

Lamont turned to Selena. "Once we get through the gate all hell's going to break loose. How are we supposed to get out of there when we're done? Whoever's left will be waiting for us."

"That's when we need a helicopter. Just for extraction."

"However we do it, we're not going to have a lot of time once we get inside," Nick said.

Nick activated the satellite link and put it on his speaker.

"Yes, Nick."

Harker's voice came through with a slight echo. An odd noise rumbled in the background.

"Director. What's that noise? It sounds like a lawnmower."

In Virginia, Elizabeth stroked the huge orange cat sprawled across her desk. He was purring. It sounded like a motorcycle engine with a carburetor problem.

"It's just Burps. Where are you with the mission planning?"

Nick told her about their idea to pose as a news crew. "We need a helicopter to get out of there."

"That's tricky," Elizabeth said.

"Lucas could set it up," Nick said. "He's itching to get even for what happened to Steph. Hood will okay it. Langley has to have something in the area. That way everything stays in house and nothing goes public. The only other option I can see is to let SOCOM in on it. Without a chopper to take us out of there it's a suicide mission."

"The last thing I want is Special Operations Command involved. Rice wouldn't like that."

"So you'll talk to Lucas?"

"I will. This will take a little time to set up. How are your quarters?"

"Impressive, if you like this sort of thing. The bed is big enough to sail to France in."

Elizabeth laughed.

Nick got serious. "When is Diego going home?"

"The plane is due at Andrews tomorrow morning. Rice had his family flown here to meet him. They're taking him to Colorado."

"He ought to be in Arlington."

"It's what his parents wanted."

"Al-Bayati has a lot to answer for," Nick said.

"I expect you to take care of that," Elizabeth said. "Out."

CHAPTER 51

The Al Jazeera van was painted with the iconic logo of the network and sported a satellite dish on the roof. Nick drove. If they were stopped it could be a problem because of his lack of Arabic but it would look suspicious if Selena was behind the wheel. She sat next to him, wearing modest clothes and a brown headscarf.

Nick had darkened his skin and applied a false beard. It was good enough to pass a quick glance. His clothes were Beirut casual. He wore a cheap striped shirt open at the collar, jeans and a shapeless jacket that concealed his pistol. An unspoken attitude completed the disguise. Ronnie and Lamont rode in the back of the van, crammed in next to a built in console used for television broadcasts.

Late afternoon sun shone through gleaming rolls of razor wire lining the top of Al-Bayati's walls, throwing twisted shadows onto the dusty street below. The street was almost empty. Whatever was happening in Syria had drawn off the Hezbollah terrorists that usually frequented the area.

Nick slowed as they approached the compound and stopped in front of the massive iron gate. One of Al-Bayati's men emerged from the guardhouse on the other side. He looked like something that had escaped from the primate cage at the zoo. He had a sloping forehead with thick black eyebrows that met in the middle and a chest that looked like something you could ride over Niagara Falls.

"Maybe we should have brought a battering ram," Lamont said.

"Or a tank," Nick said. "You ready, Selena?"

"Alihya Kalil, budding journalist, at your service."

"What's Alihya mean?"

"The exalted, of the highest social standing, so watch your manners."

"Yes, your Majesty."

Selena got out of the van and walked over to the gate

"As-salamu alayka," she said.

"As-salamu alayki," the guard responded. "You are the journalist here to interview? You are not expected until this afternoon." He regarded Selena with suspicion. "I watch Al Jazeera all the time. I haven't seen you before."

Selena handed a card through the gate with her name and the Al Jazeera logo on it. A white plastic ID card with her picture and official seal hung on a chain around her neck. She held it up for him to see.

"I'm new. This is my first big assignment." She turned to the van and gestured. Ronnie got out of the back with a camera. He was dressed like Nick.

"I'd like to start the piece with some background shots with you in them," Selena said. "Then I'd like to ask you a few questions. Is that all right? It's a responsible position, protecting such an important man."

"Yes, it is." The guard puffed himself up. "An important post. Al-Bayati relies on me."

Ronnie put the camera to his shoulder and aimed it at the guard. He looked through the lens and turned it on. The guard looked through the grill work of the gate at the red light, thinking how his image would soon be seen by millions.

Selena turned to Ronnie and held up her hand to stop, telling him in Arabic that the gate was in the way of the shot. He had no idea what she'd said but the hand signal was clear enough. He lowered the camera.

"Could you please open the gate for us?"

She smiled at the guard.

He retreated to the shack and threw a switch. The gate rolled slowly to the side. Nick put the van in gear and drove into the compound. Once they were clear, the guard toggled the switch and the gate closed behind them.

Showtime, Nick thought.

He reached down by the seat, laid an MP5 across his lap and clicked off the safety. All his senses were on high alert. He looked through the windshield of the van and took in the large courtyard, the steps to the entrance of the villa, the lethal shape of the half track with the Quad .50. The weapon was unmanned, the four deadly barrels at rest and pointed toward the sky. Several guards lounged in the shade at the front of the villa. He cracked his door open.

Nick watched Selena and the guard in his mirror.

"I need to look inside your van," the guard said. He began walking toward the truck.

"Get ready," Nick said to Lamont. "Go when I open the door. One talking to Selena and heading this way. Three in front of the house. They're watching to see what's happening. No one's on the Quad."

"One piece of good news."

"Now."

Nick kicked the door open with his foot and came out facing the villa. Behind him, the back doors of the van banged open as Lamont piled out. The men at the villa started to stand. Nick fired a quick three round burst, then a second. Ronnie dropped the camera, took an MP5 from under his jacket and shot the guard.

Nick's first burst had taken down one of the men in front of the villa. The other two scrambled for their weapons. One of them brought up an AK and got off a burst. The bullets racketed against the metal side of the van, punching holes through the Al Jazeera logo. Lamont shot him. The last man never made it to his weapon before Ronnie put two rounds in him.

Selena reached into the truck and took another MP5 from the back. The four of them ran toward the villa entrance. A man appeared in the doorway. Lamont and Nick fired and he fell away out of sight.

Then they were through the door and inside the house. They found themselves in a large atrium with a tiled floor and a tiered fountain in the middle. Streams of clear water spouted up and fell back into the basins with a pleasant sound. After the heat outside, the room was cool and comfortable. Seven lamps with elaborate metal shades hung from the ceiling far overhead. A staircase made of flowery white and yellow tiles rose to the second floor and a balcony held up by columns of white stone. A carved stone railing followed the balcony around the sides of the atrium. Doors to more rooms were visible on the second story. Huge painted urns holding flowering trees were spaced at intervals around the ground floor of the atrium.

Two men came out of a side room firing AKs on full auto. Nick dove for cover behind one of the planters. The bullets smashed into the pot, shaking loose a rain of red blossoms and showering him with dirt. More AK rounds went by, sounding their distinctive, deadly whine. Guards emerged on the balcony above and began shooting down into the atrium.

The air filled with chips of tile and spent bullets ricocheting around the open space. The atrium echoed with the harsh explosions of the guns and the clatter of empty shell casings bouncing on the hard floor.

Nick leaned around the pot and shot one of the men on the balcony. The body fell over the railing and landed headfirst with a dull sound like a watermelon breaking.

Nick ducked back. "The ones on the ground floor are dead."

Selena crouched behind one of the urns. She tore the scarf from her head and dropped it on the floor. Her expression was tightlipped, grim.

He called over the noise of the gunfire. "Lamont, you and Selena cover. Ronnie, you and me, up the stairs."

Ronnie nodded.

"Go."

Lamont and Selena knelt and began a steady rain of fire at the men on the second floor. The value of automatic weapons wasn't in their accuracy. It was in keeping enemies from shooting back while someone else closed on them. Nick ran for the stair with Ronnie on his heels, firing up as he went. Pieces of stone chipped away from the balustrade. A bullet grazed his thigh like a quick razor burn. He tripped and went down. Ronnie went past him on the stair. Nick ejected, jammed in a new magazine and shot another man on the balcony.

Suddenly it was quiet. After the racket of the guns, the stillness felt alien. Nick climbed to his feet.

"You all right?" Ronnie stood next to him.

"Yeah." He looked down at the bloody rip in his jeans. "Just a scratch."

Selena and Lamont came up the stairs.

"We have to clear the second floor," Nick said. "I don't want any surprises. Selena, close the front doors and watch the entrance. We don't have much time. All that noise is going to bring someone."

"The gate is closed," Selena said. "That will slow them up."

"For a while."

A few minutes later Nick, Ronnie and Lamont came back down the steps.

"Nobody there."

"The front entrance is barred and the doors are solid," Selena said. "No one's getting through without us knowing about it."

They looked through the rooms on the ground floor. There was no sign of Al-Bayati.

"He has to be here," Selena said.

They found one more door at the end of a hall.

"The other side of that door is the only place left," Lamont said.

"Then let's go find the son of a bitch."

Nick opened the door.

CHAPTER 52

The door was heavy, thick, like a bank vault door. Beyond it, a flight of stairs descended to a passage below. Yellow light flickered from somewhere beyond.

"Kind of overkill for a house door," Lamont said. "It looks like it belongs in a bank."

"Soundproof," Selena said. "You could set off a bomb behind that and no one would hear it."

Nick rubbed his ear. "If Al-Bayati is down there, he might not know we're here. I don't think he could have heard the guns."

A stale odor hung in the air.

"What's that smell?" Selena said.

Ronnie sniffed. "Fire. Something else."

"Like someone's been barbecuing," Lamont said.

They went down the stairs without seeing anyone. The light grew brighter as they neared the bottom. A short hallway led from the last step into a large room. It took a few seconds for Nick to realize what he was looking at. When the meaning sank in he knew he would carry the sight with him for the rest of his life.

The room was lit with tall wax candles. Fire leapt from a large, round brazier of black iron mounted on a tripod. The floor of the chamber was made of polished cedar. The flames from the brazier and the candles filled the room with a fiery glow. Beyond the brazier was a fat, gilded statue depicting a standing horned god with an erect phallus. He had the body of a man and the head of a bull. The animal face was contorted with a terrible smile. The arms were held out on the other side of the flaming brazier, with the palms up and the hands slanted down.

Al-Bayati stood to the side of the flames, his back toward them. He was dressed in a floor length robe of deep blue. A shawl of the same material covered his head. His hands were raised in supplication toward the statue and he was chanting, the words like snakes slithering through dry grass. On his left hand he wore the ring of Solomon. In his right he held a bundle of herbs.

Next to Al-Bayati was the ugly man, Badr. Neither of the two had seen them. Nick would have shot them both from where he stood except that Badr held a child in his arms, a girl of about nine or ten years. Her body was limp, unconscious. Her hair hung perilously close to the flames.

Selena grasped Nick's arm. "That's Moloch. They're going to sacrifice that child to Moloch."

At the sound of her voice, Al-Bayati and Badr turned toward them. Bayati's face was strangely calm. He smiled and threw the bundle of herbs onto the brazier. A cloud of black and white smoke rose like a poisonous mushroom, releasing a thick, sweet scent.

His eyes glittered.

"He's stoned out of his mind," Lamont said.

"Carter," Al-Bayati said. "I wouldn't come any closer if I were you."

Nick gestured with his MP5. "Away from the fire. You too, big man."

"Take a step and the child dies," Al-Bayati said. "Badr."

Badr handed the girl to him. Al-Bayati moved close and held the child over the hands of the idol.

"It's simple," he said. "I put the child into the hands of the god and she slides off into the flames. The body contracts and creates the most wonderful smile as he welcomes her."

"You're sick," Nick said.

Bayati's expression changed. "I am the high priest of Moloch, as my ancestors have been before me for centuries. Even Solomon built a Temple to him when he recognized his power. Be careful how you speak in the presence of the god."

Ronnie was moving slowly to the side. Badr watched him.

"Did Solomon use that ring when he built it?" Selena asked.

She was trying to buy time. Nick couldn't see how he could get the child away from Al-Bayati before the girl went into the fire.

"You begin to understand. Yes, he invoked the jinn to help him."

"I would like to see that," Selena said, "the jinn."

"Oh, I doubt that. Besides, they seldom make themselves visible in our dimension."

"You've seen them. Tell me, what do they look like?"

For the first time, Al-Bayati seemed uncertain.

"They have not yet chosen to appear for me. After the sacrifice they will come."

"They only come if they are summoned by the ring," Selena said. "It won't work if you don't pronounce the incantations correctly."

"How would you know about these things?"

"Don't you know who I am? I'm an expert in these languages. I may be the only person alive who can speak them with the right inflection. Just now you were chanting in one of the Western Punic dialects from ancient Carthage. I could tell that it wasn't right."

Al-Bayati's eyes widened. "A guess."

"No."

"Tell your man to stop moving or the child dies."

"Ronnie, stop," Nick said.

Ronnie froze.

Badr smiled through his rotten teeth. His eyes were all pupil, black in the firelight.

He's stoned too, Nick thought.

"They'll never come unless you use the right words," Selena said.

"Then you will help me call them," Al-Bayati said. "If they appear, the child will live. If you fail, she dies. As will you and your friends."

He's lying, she thought.

"Give me your oath as the high priest of Moloch that you will keep your word."

"I swear," Al-Bayati said. "And you must swear to obey me. Do as I say or I give the girl to the god."

"I swear it."

"Selena..."

"Nick, I want to see the jinn. I'll never have another chance."

"Are you nuts?" Lamont said.

"Woman, come here. Badr, watch them."

Badr went to a carved wooden cabinet set to the side of the statue. He took out a Skorpion machine pistol and pointed it at them. Selena began walking toward the idol.

Nick didn't believe for a second that she wanted to see the jinn. What mattered was that Al-Bayati in his drugged state believed it. There would only be one chance to save the child. His ear began to itch with a fierce burning sensation.

"Where are the writings?" Selena asked.

"In a drawer on the top of the cabinet. Be careful, woman. Moloch's hands are slippery."

"If you drop her I won't help you call the jinn."

Al-Bayati watched as she opened the drawer and took out a piece of yellowed vellum covered with writing in black ink. It was in a language she had never seen. She glanced over at Nick and saw him catch the look. It was now or never.

"Begin," Al-Bayati commanded.

Selena held the parchment up as if to start reading. With a sudden motion she threw it into the fire. The vellum burst into a flare of bright yellow flame. Before Al-Bayati could react she knocked the girl out of his hands and body-slammed him into the brazier. He went down on the floor as the brazier toppled over, showering him with red hot coals. He screamed as they struck his face. His robe caught fire.

Nick, Ronnie and Lamont opened fire at Badr. A dozen rounds staggered him. He crumpled to the floor.

Al-Bayati writhed on the floor, screaming, his robe burning. He struggled to his feet, enveloped in flame. He stumbled into the golden idol and fell to the floor. The screams were horrible.

Nick shot him. The screaming stopped. The room filled with the stench of burning flesh as the robe smoldered.

"I guess that's what you call poetic justice," Lamont said.

Ronnie went over to the body. He took a bandana from his pocket and pulled Solomon's ring off Al-Bayati's dead finger, wiped it clean and wrapped the cloth around it.

"Here." He gave it to Nick.

Selena knelt by the girl and picked her up. She stirred, unconscious.

"She's drugged and took a hit from the floor when I knocked her out of his hands. I think she's all right."

"We'll take her with us," Nick said.

"Could you really understand what Al-Bayati was saying?" Ronnie asked Selena. "When he was chanting?"

"Not a word. I haven't a clue."

The wood floor began to burn where the coals had fallen on it. Nick tried the comm link. "There's no signal down here. Come on."

They went back upstairs. Nick tried again.

"Nick. What's happening?" Elizabeth's voice was tense.

"We're inside Bayati's villa. We have the ring and Bayati's dead. Where's our ride?"

"Offshore, waiting for your signal."

"Send him in."

Selena went to the door and listened.

"Nick. I hear people shouting."

"Director, we may have a problem outside. How soon will that chopper be here?"

"I just signaled, they're on the way. Five minutes, no more."

"Tell him to land in the courtyard in front of the villa. Tell him he might take hostile fire."

"Copy that."

"Tell him we'll give him covering fire if he needs it."

"Nick, those are civilians out there."

"I don't think so," Nick said. "This is Hezbollah territory and nobody gives a damn about what happens to Al-Bayati except them. Anyone out there is hostile."

"Be sure about that before you start shooting."

"Out," Nick said. He broke the connection.

"She has a point," Selena said.

"They don't shoot at us, we won't shoot at them. Whatever we do, they'll lie about it."

He took the bar from the front door. They could hear the shouts getting louder.

"It sounds like they're on the other side of the gate," Ronnie said.

He cracked open the door and looked through the opening. A burst of automatic fire sent splinters from the frame. Ronnie shut the door.

"Not civilians."

"I figured that out," Nick said. "That makes things easier. You know how to run that Quad .50?"

"Nope."

"I do," Lamont said. "We still had a few on riverboats in the SEALS."

"I'm thinking that when our ride arrives we use it to discourage the crowd until we can get out of here."

"There are supposed to be two loaders and a gunner on that unit," Lamont said. "Each of those magazines holds two hundred rounds. They disappear pretty quick once the shooting starts. We don't even know if it's loaded."

"It's a chance we have to take. I don't think Al-Bayati would have it there just for show."

"I hope they kept the batteries charged."

"You won't be on it long. One burst from that and we won't have to worry about that crowd. We just need enough time to let the chopper pick us up."

"Better let him know what we're doing. I don't want someone in that bird to think I'm one of the bad guys."

Nick called Harker.

"Your ride is almost there, Nick."

"Director, we're going to have to shoot our way out of here." He looked at the ceiling. "I hear the bird coming," Nick said. "We're going to be busy for the next few minutes."

"I'm switching you over to the helicopter now. Your call sign is Delta One."

"Copy that."

A new voice came on line.

"Delta One, this is Blazer. Looks like you have a problem."

"Blazer, Delta One. You see that Quad .50 in the courtyard?"

"Copy that. I have it locked in."

"Negative, Blazer. Do not take it out. Do not take it out. We need it to disperse the hostiles."

"Copy," the pilot said. "Ready when you are, One."

"We're coming out the front door now. There are four of us and a child."

"Copy that."

"Lamont, we'll lay down fire while you get to the gun. It's only about twenty feet. Clear that gate."

"I'm a little slow," Lamont said. "Y'all have to run interference for me."

Nick patted his MP5. "That's what we've got these for. We'll go in front of you and keep them busy. Once we get to the half track it will give us cover. Selena, you take the girl."

He stood by the entrance. "Ready? Let's do it."

Nick pulled open the door. Someone started shooting at the front of the house, the bullets making small craters in the whitewashed stucco wall of the villa. They ran toward the half track, firing toward the gate. Lamont clambered up onto the seat of the Quad .50, settling in behind an armored shield that protected the lower part of his body. Two more flat plates added protection to each side of the sight. If someone put a round between them he was a dead man. Jacketed bullets rang off the steel armor like hard rain. Lamont flipped the red guard over the activating switch and whispered a quick prayer for charged batteries.

The Quad .50 had been designed as a mobile antiaircraft gun in World War II. No longer useful against modern jet aircraft, it had been reborn as an antipersonnel weapon in the European and Pacific theaters. In Vietnam the guns had been mounted on patrol boats moving up and down the Mekong.

The weapon was mounted on a swivel base, controlled by two handles in front of the gunner. Pushing forward on both brought the four barrels down and pulling back took them up. Pushing the left handle forward rotated the gun clockwise. Pushing on the right handle turned it to the left. Lamont pushed forward, swiveled left and brought the guns to bear on the gate.

He fired. The air filled with smoke and a cloud of empty cases flying into the air.

The noise of four .50 caliber Browning machine guns firing at once was beyond deafening. The heavy bullets shattered against the metal grill work, knocking off pieces of iron and shredding the Hezbollah soldiers on the other side. It tore them apart, filling the air with blood and pieces of flesh. The weapon had earned the nickname of the "meat chopper" in World War II. Lamont watched what the gun did to the people beyond the gate and understood why.

The ammunition drums emptied and the gun stopped. Hundreds of empty shells littered the stones. The air stank of cordite. A haze of smoke hung over the courtyard.

The others were already climbing on board the helicopter. Nick and Ronnie grabbed Lamont's arms and pulled him into the bay as the pilot lifted away. He looked down at the destruction he had caused and the shattered bodies lying in the street on the other side of the gate. His coffee colored skin was pale.

"That's one bad ass weapon," he said. "I never want to use one again."

The helicopter banked out over the blue Mediterranean and headed for safety.

Behind them, flames broke through the roof of Al-Bayati's villa.

CHAPTER 53

Diego's file was on Elizabeth's desk. She looked at her team, sitting across from her desk. They seemed subdued, Lamont in particular.

Stephanie was almost ready to come in. Joe Eggleston had gone back to Langley.

Elizabeth picked up Solomon's ring and studied it.

"He really thought this could call beings from another dimension?"

Selena nodded. "He was insane. I don't think he cared much about the things from the Temple. Just the ring."

Lamont rubbed his leg. "You wouldn't have believed it, Director. That statue was the creepiest thing I've seen outside of a horror movie. He was going to burn that little girl alive."

"I'm not sorry I missed it. The important thing is that you stopped him."

"He'd probably been doing it for years," Nick said, "sacrificing children to that thing."

"He won't be doing it anymore," Elizabeth said. "This is one we can chalk up in the plus column."

"What are you going to do with the ring?" Selena asked.

"Give it back. Rice has decided to send the ring to Jerusalem. Everything else in that cave is being claimed by both Ethiopia and the Israelis. It will take years to straighten it out."

"Those things should go back to Jerusalem," Selena said.

"I agree with you," Elizabeth said, "but this involves religion and politics, not to mention gold. That makes it complicated."

"What else is new?" Lamont said.

"There's going to be fallout from what happened in Beirut," Elizabeth said. "Hezbollah's creatures in the Lebanese government are claiming the people you killed outside that gate were peaceful civilians. They want whoever was responsible tried for war crimes."

"Figures," Nick said. "They're good at accusing everybody else of the things they do."

"They don't know who it was," Elizabeth said. "The helicopter was unmarked. They assume it was us or the Israelis. It's not going to go anywhere, especially when the story gets out about what Al-Bayati was doing in there."

"The story will get out?"

"You can be sure of it."

"Director, I've been thinking," Lamont said. "Retirement isn't what it's cracked up to be. Besides, there's too many damn bugs down there in Florida. I'd like to get my old job back, if I could."

"What about your leg?"

"It held up pretty good this time around. Better than I thought it would, and it's getting stronger. I don't think it's going to be a problem."

Elizabeth looked at Nick.

"He's pretty beat up and he's getting old," Nick said. "I guess we could use him."

"I wouldn't talk about old if I were you," Lamont said.

Elizabeth smiled. "Welcome back."

Selena changed the subject. "How's Stephanie doing?"

"I talked to her this morning. It's going to take time to get over losing the baby. She wants to work as soon as she feels physically okay. She's tough and she knows she can have another child when she's ready. She'll be all right."

"This has been a rough one," Nick said. "Stephanie. Then Diego. He just got here and then he was gone. There was nothing we could do."

Elizabeth opened a drawer in her desk and took out a bottle of cognac and some shot glasses. They watched while she filled the glasses. They all took one, even Ronnie. She filled one more glass and set it down on Diego's file.

"There is one thing we can do, for him and all the others who have given their lives because of duty. We can honor their memory." She raised her glass. "Nick?"

They lifted their glasses.

"To Diego," Nick said. "A good man."

Epilogue

The weather was warm for October, one of those gorgeous days when summer made a brief reappearance before the approach of another brutal East Coast winter.

Nick and Selena came out of the chapel to a shower of rice from their friends. They stopped for the photographer to take shots as they left the church. Ronnie, Lamont, Lucas, Stephanie and Elizabeth came after them, followed by Clarence Hood with his security detail. The president had been unable to attend. He'd sent his regrets and a gift and wished them well.

"You're beautiful in that dress," Nick said.

Selena kissed him. "You look pretty good yourself. A tuxedo suits you. You know, it's the first time I've seen you dressed up like that."

"I haven't worn a tux since my high school prom."

Elizabeth came over to them. "The limo is waiting. Security is getting nervous standing out here like this."

Nick looked around. "Just for once I'd like to think I could have a normal day like everybody else. Especially this day."

They walked toward the car, a white Rolls-Royce with a uniformed chauffeur. He held the rear door open for Selena. On the smooth leather seat was a package wrapped in white paper with a white bow. An envelope was stuck under the bow. He could make out part of what was written on the envelope.

To my...

"Where did that come from?" Nick asked. His ear began itching.

"I don't know, sir."

"Have you been with the car all the time?"

"I did take a short break for a call of nature, sir."

"Are you English?"

"As a matter of fact, I am, sir. They like to use me as the driver when a client requests the Rolls. Is something the matter, sir?"

Lucas came over.

"Hey, you guys are supposed to be on your way to the reception. Everybody's waiting."

"Someone put a package in the back of the car," Selena said.

"There goes normal," Nick said. "Lucas, move everyone back will you? Selena, you too."

"Nick..."

"I've got a bad feeling about it."

"It's probably a toaster."

"It's too big for a toaster."

The itch was turning into a slow burn. Nick tugged on his ear and looked at the package, wondering what was inside. Even on his wedding day he had to worry about people trying to kill him. It pissed him off.

"I think it's a bomb," Nick said. His voice was quiet.

"Okay," Lucas said.

"You're pretty cool."

"I'm a fatalist. How do you want to handle it?"

"We all back off. If it is a bomb, there could be somebody watching us right now with a detonator."

"Waiting for you and Selena to get in the car," Lucas said.

"You're full of cheerful ideas, aren't you?"

"You're the one who thinks it's a bomb."

Clarence Hood and Elizabeth were on the steps of the church looking at them, wondering what the delay was about.

Nick turned to Selena. "Let's stroll over toward the photographer and tell him we want some more shots with the wedding party. If someone's watching and they see us moving away for more pictures it will look natural. Assuming it's a bomb and not a toaster, that is. And smile, will you? Laugh a little."

Nick took her arm and steered her back toward the church. He saw the chauffeur. His name tag said that his name was James.

"Lucas, get everybody back into the church. I have an idea."

He stopped by the chauffeur. "Is there a phone in the car?"

"Yes, sir, there is. It's used to contact me if the owner wishes to advise me of traffic or a change in plan."

"Good. Come with us into the church."

"Very good, sir."

If the chauffeur thought this particular wedding party was acting a little bizarre, he put it down to the increased security surrounding the Director of Central Intelligence. It was all rather exciting, something different from the normal wedding or evening hire.

They went inside the church and Nick closed the heavy oaken doors. Everyone moved up toward the altar.

"Mister Carter..."

"Don't worry, Reverend. Everyone, there may be a bomb in the car. Get behind something. James, does that Rolls have a remote start?"

James looked indignant, as if anything could be missing from a Rolls-Royce.

"Of course, sir."

"Start the car."

James took out his key and pressed a button. The car started, although it was hard to tell it was running.

"Good. Now call the phone in the car for me."

The chauffeur took out his cell phone and dialed the number.

In the street outside, the Rolls vanished in an explosion that shook the stone walls of the church and set the bells in the tower ringing. The force of the blast blew the stained glass out of the front of the church and shook the heavy doors.

Dust drifted down from the rafters of the church, settling on Nick's tuxedo. He brushed it off his shoulder.

The Reverend picked himself up from the floor. "Good God," he said.

"How did you know?" Lucas asked.

"I didn't, except when my ear starts burning like that it means trouble. I figured that since it didn't go off when the car started, it wasn't set on an ignition or movement trigger. I think someone was waiting down the road and watching. All they had to do was dial that number when it went by."

Selena took his hand. "Bastards. This is our wedding day. Our day. Who would do this?"

"I don't know," Nick said, "but I'm going to find out."

New Releases...

Be the first to know when I have a new book coming out by subscribing to my newsletter. No spam or busy emails, only a brief announcement now and then. Just click on the link below. You can unsubscribe at any time...

http://alexlukeman.com/contact.html#newsletter

The Project Series

White Jade
The Lance
The Seventh Pillar
Black Harvest
The Tesla Secret
The Nostradamus File
The Ajax Protocol
The Eye of Shiva
Black Rose
The Solomon Scroll

Reviews and comments by readers are welcome!

You can contact me at: alex@alexlukeman.com.
I promise to get back to you.

My website is: www.alexlukeman.com

Acknowledgments

Gayle, who believes in me, a necessary condition for being a writer and for my overall peace of mind.

Special thanks to Seth Ballard, Gloria Lakritz, Paul Madsen, Eric Vollebregt, Nancy Witt. Your keen eyes made this a much better book.

Neil Jackson for a classic action cover.

Notes

The Project books take advantage of developments in weapons technology that may sound futuristic but are far from fictional, like the stealth helicopter used to penetrate Saudi Arabian airspace. These helicopters exist. It might have been one of these that was destroyed during the raid on Osama bin Laden's compound in Pakistan.

Onyx is also real, a sophisticated satellite ground penetrating radar system which surpasses anything else of its kind anywhere in the world. You can bet that the Pentagon is using it to scan for underground sites where rogue governments and potential enemies might be hiding something nasty.

The Kord heavy machine gun used by Al-Bayati's mercenaries is a good example of the developing sophistication of Russian weapons. It's rugged, light, accurate up to 2000 meters and fires a devastating 12.7 X 108 mm cartridge. It has the unique advantage of being light enough to mount on a bipod as an individual infantry weapon. There are many other weapons in the modern Russian arsenal as good or possibly better than anything in our own but I'll leave those for another time.

Moloch, or his alter ego, Baal, was a principle male god of the Carthaginians. There is significant evidence to indicate that human sacrifices were offered to him. The name Baal later morphed into Beelzelbub.

My apologies to the scientific world for destroying one of the great achievements of modern science, the European Synchrotron Radiation Facility at Grenoble. The scrolls of the Villa Literati in Herculaneum exist are one of the intriguing mysteries of the ancient world. Crystal x-ray tomography is an advanced technique developed at the facility. It has recently been used to begin unraveling the secrets of the ash encrusted scrolls, just as described in the book.

The remains of Solomon have never been found and identified. There is still much controversy over whether or not he actually existed. My personal preference is to believe that he did and that the story of the Queen of Sheba's visit found in the Old Testament is very likely based on actual events. The line identifying Sheba on her ossuary in the Ethiopian shrine comes from the *Song of Solomon*, one of the great love poems of all time.

About the Author

Alex Lukeman writes action/adventure thrillers featuring a covert intelligence unit called the PROJECT and is the author of the award-winning Amazon best seller, *The Tesla Secret*. Alex is a former Marine and psychotherapist. He uses his experience of the military and human nature to inform his work. He likes riding old, fast motorcycles and playing guitar, usually not at the same time. You can email him at alex@alexlukeman.com. He loves hearing from readers and promises he will get back to you.

Made in the USA
Middletown, DE
23 June 2018